TALES
OF THE
SLUG

edited by
Brianne DiMarco

BLUE FRGE PRESS
Port Orchard, Washington

Blue Forge Press is the print division of the volunteer-run, federal 501(c)3 nonprofit company, Blue Legacy, founded in 1989 and dedicated to bringing light to the shadows and voice to the silence. We strive to empower storytellers across all walks of life with our four divisions: Blue Forge Press, Blue Forge Films, Blue Forge Gaming, and Blue Forge Records. Find out more at www.MyBlueLegacy.com

Blue Forge Press
7419 Ebbert Drive Southeast
Port Orchard, Washington 98367
blueforgepress@gmail.com
360-550-2071 ph.txt

to all those, young and old alike,
who delight in the weird and the wondrous
creatures of our planet

Table of Contents

TALES
OF THE
SLUG

edited by
Brianne DiMarco

The Gastropod Patriot March

Andrew Dolbeck

The whole nasty business was, of course, completely unfair to the slugs.

After it was over, Jenny made a convalescent garden for the survivors, ringed with leafy edible plants. She felt it was the least she could do. She was appalled by how quickly things got out of hand.

"War," her husband said, "always involves soldiers dying for the interests of their leaders." Jenny supposed that he must be right. Ron had a knack of seeing the world clearly while she was always confounded by seeing the worlds that might be, could be, almost are, and should maybe have been.

Habitual apartment dwellers before marriage, Ron and Jenny had decided to try a house in the suburbs after the wedding. A place that would *theirs*, not merely hers or his. They found a nice little two-story fixer-upper just north of the city limits. It had a postage stamp of a lawn, ringed by flowerbeds along side an honest-to-God white picket fence.

Ron liked the place because he got to grumble about all the work that needed to be done around the place. Jenny liked the house for its peculiar *houseness*. It was a home, but a home built by human hands using wood and nails and gypsum and paint. Jenny loved to run her fingers along the walls in different rooms. They had different textures. The brick stonework by the fireplace was rough beneath her fingers and felt old and sturdy, a little more cantankerous than friendly, but solid and enduring. The eggshell white plasterboard walls of the bedroom felt smooth and just slightly yielding, like skin over hard muscle. The front entryway had a rough wood finish, old-fashioned but warm and welcoming.

The rooms had smells, too. Musty and dusty storage spaces, the crisp scent of old ash near the fireplace, the smell of new carpet in the main room. Ron only grumbled more when Jenny tried to tell him about the smells. He didn't think houses were supposed to smell. Jenny didn't see why not. Everything else in the world had smells.

The house also had neighbors. In particular it had Mr. Shotze. Mr. Shotze had the largest, oldest, and most grand house in the neighborhood. Mr. Shotze's house had a huge, elaborate, landscaped garden, carefully manicured and maintained. Mr. Shotze loved his garden.

His grand house also had a telescope on the upper terrace, which he said was for amateur astronomy. Jenny knew that meant looking at the stars. She always preferred to listen to the stars, but Ron assured her that no one else could hear them.

It might be worth mentioning that Jenny was not like other people. She was one of the four most powerful witches in the world. Jenny heard the stars on quiet nights, saw mermaids in the play of light on water, and talked to good dreams so that they would visit the people she cared about while they slept. Some days the magic made her delirious, seeing the world through a fevered haze. Even on her good days, Jenny knew that she saw the world differently from everyone else. She remembered things that never happened. Forgot things that needed to be done. Living with her was difficult some times, but Ron never complained. She knew he loved her. It was as simple and impossible as that.

On the first anniversary of her marriage, Jenny had decided to surprise her husband with a slinky little number she bought in one of those stores that her parents told her good little girls never went into. She held the outfit up in front of her. It had lots of frilly lace, but little else. Jenny liked lace. She hoped Ron would like the little else. As she was undressing, she happened to notice that Mr. Shotze's telescope was not pointed at the heavens, but at her bedroom window. Mr. Shotze, his eye squinting into the thing, didn't seem to notice her noticing him. He probably wasn't looking at her face. The curtains should have been closed, but they were not. And wasn't that just like curtains?

Jenny stood blushing, frozen in a moment of indecision—flee the room? Yank the curtains closed? She wasn't about to put on a show. Not for Mr. Shotze. This moment was for Ron, who had earned it with his daily patience. She had no desire to share it with anyone else. Finally, she glared at the curtains until they got the hint and closed themselves.

She didn't tell Ron. She wanted him to enjoy their anniversary. For the most part, they both had a wonderful evening filled with fine food, candles, and red wine. Ron grinned as he watched the dancing silverware show that Jenny had spent the morning choreographing. The salad forks kept losing the beat, but overall she thought it wasn't bad for an amateur production. But at odd moments, creepy thoughts of Mr. Shotze and his telescope intruded on Jenny's peace of mind, jarring her away from the pleasures of the moment. When, at the end of it all, they retreated to the bedroom, Ron didn't ask why the curtains had been nailed shut, and Jenny didn't volunteer the information.

She didn't sleep well that night. She dreamed that the walls of the house had turned against her. The bedroom walls just up and left, muttering amongst themselves. The wood walls of the entry hall turned themselves to glass, so that every one who passed by on the street could look into the house. Only the sturdy brick of the fireplace held fast to its duty. Someone had to hold on to the roof, after all. Otherwise it might get ideas.

The next day, Jenny carefully checked each wall in the house, reassuring herself over and over that it had only been a dream. She even asked Ron if he'd seen the walls going away last night. He told her that he'd felt the earth move, but he hadn't noticed anything particular about the walls. Jenny spent the afternoon wandering around the house in a daze. She felt like something had been taken from her, but she couldn't put a name to just what it was.

And then she realized that she no longer trusted the house she loved. It was silly, she thought. The house hadn't betrayed her. Someone else had taken that simple faith away from her. Mr. Shotze.

After that, her thoughts turned toward revenge. She decided to spoil Mr. Shotze's enjoyment of what he loved. And that meant attacking his garden.

Jenny searched around her tiny garden strip. It

didn't take long for her to find what she wanted. Slugs. There was a lovely trio of the slimy things curled over the artichoke leaves. Jenny addressed them politely and immediately began to speak in praise of the wonders of Mr. Shotze's garden.

Yes, the slugs agreed, *it sounds grand. But it is so far away. A slug is happiest wherever a slug already is.*

Jenny thought about that for a moment. Did it follow that a slug could not actually be happier if it were somewhere else? She tried again, telling them that Mr. Shotze's garden was, in fact, nothing short of the lost slug Paradise of ancient legend. The slugs had every right to reclaim it.

That did the trick. The slugs not only turned their eyestalks towards Mr. Shotze's yard, they also spread the word. They left codes in their slime trails and whispered in the night to other slugs they passed on their long pilgrimage.

Within a week, Mr. Shotze's garden was infested. He responded with slug bait poisons and little cardboard pest traps. One morning, Jenny went out for the paper and noticed that there were over a dozen slugs lined up at the edge of her garden, gazing wistfully across the property line at Mr. Shotze's garden. *Paradise has become tainted,* they told her. *We must be unworthy.*

Jenny thought about that for a moment. She told

the slugs that they must have faith. Paradise was worth a little adversity. The traps only weeded out the unbelievers. The faithful would yet thrive.

As one, the slugs began their slimy march back toward Paradise. As before, the word spread, and within days, Mr. Shotze's garden had more slugs than any garden in the neighborhood.

As before, Mr. Shotze responded with poisons and traps. He added a high-pressure garden hose to his arsenal. And when he had his garden relatively clear of slugs, he ringed its border with a thick line of rock salt.

We have fallen, the slugs told Jenny. *We are lost from Paradise.*

Jenny thought about that for a moment. She told the slugs that it was their duty to reclaim Paradise. The task might require sacrifices, but future generations of slugs, secure in Paradise, would honor the fallen. It was time now for courage, for acts of valor and determination.

The slugs listened intently. When Jenny was finished, they conferred briefly among themselves. Then they left, all sliding on their slime trails in different directions. Not one headed for Mr. Shotze's garden. Jenny sighed quietly to herself. Well, it had been worth a try. She wasn't wholly satisfied with her revenge on Mr. Shotze, but time had dimmed the insult. She supposed it would have to do.

But the slugs hadn't given up. It took weeks for the slug army to assemble. Many smaller neighborhood gardens were destroyed in the army's march from its gathering places towards Paradise. Armies, like slugs, travel on their stomachs.

It was a Sunday morning. Jenny stepped out for the morning newspaper. She liked the Sunday paper. It had the color funnies. When she saw them, she forgot the paper entirely. A gray-silver carpet, moving by inches, stretched across the street. There were hundreds of them.

It took them an hour to reach the salt barrier. Jenny stood silent, watching. Mr. Shotze had maintained the barrier, refreshing it after every rain, checking it for breaches every few days. He was serious about defending his garden. The line of salt was solid, nearly a full slug-width wide, and circled unbroken around the entire circumference of Paradise.

The slugs did not hesitate. The first line threw their bodies onto the corrosive white crystals. Behind them, the second wave continued to advance. Slugs oozing over slugs, the army pressed forward over the bodies of its fallen. The salt took many of the second line, and a few of the third, but wave after wave the slugs advanced.

A slug is happiest wherever a slug is, Jenny remembered, watching the forward march in horror and awe.

Soon, the entire south side of Mr. Shotze's garden was as gray as it had ever been green. The side door of his elegant house slammed open and the man himself raced out, his loose bathrobe flopping open to reveal boxer shorts covered with pictures of little red chili peppers. Mr. Shotze gripped a broom in one white-knuckled hand. His face was red and flushed. He sputtered incomprehensibly as he swung the broom about. It did no good—for every slug he dislodged, a dozen took its place.

Hearing the commotion, Ron stepped out into the carport, a mug of steaming coffee in his hand. "What's going on?" he asked. He followed Jenny's gaze, turning to look across the carport at the neighboring house. "Jenny? Is there something you'd like to tell me?"

She told him the whole sordid story.

"That's horrible," he said, when she had finished.

"Is it?" she asked.

"All those slugs. . . ." Ron shook his head. "And it has nothing to do with Paradise. You just made that up."

"I thought it was clever," Jenny said. She wasn't so certain now.

"They're out there on their grand march, and they don't even know that it's really about you and Mr. Shotze."

Jenny thought about that for a moment. It had been easy to tell the slugs anything she thought would help her cause. It never occurred to her to tell them to attack Mr. Shotze because he was a nasty little voyeur. After all, the slugs would have just told her that was her problem. And they would have been right.

"Should I stop them?" she asked Ron.

He took a moment to watch the red-faced man failing about with the broom. "Well," he said at last. "It's a little late for that now. I'm going to go inside and grab my camera." He turned toward the house and then looked back to his wife. "Next time, though? Just call the police."

Things settled out, as they always do, eventually. Over time, Mr. Shotze reclaimed his garden, if not his peace of mind. Jenny forgave him his indiscretion, although she kept the bedroom curtains nailed shut. She and Ron had more anniversaries, often with more traditional gifts. Life goes on.

And in their convalescent garden, a new generation of slugs whispered conspiratorially amongst themselves, occasionally turning their eyestalks to gaze across the carport to the forbidden fruits of Paradise.

Ario Limax's Last Report

Alan Searle

The barrier had been breached. Well, if not exactly breached, it seemed that one of the grunts from J Division had ignored the warnings, fallen from the cross-piece, and landed on the copper. Maybe he could have made it out, but he would have been "electrolytically challenged," and probably crippled, for the rest of his life. It seemed he had held on, and now his body was oozing its juices over the strip where he had decided to stay.

Body hopping, as we call it in Q Division, was not the best way to get to the goal, but it could be done if you were quick about it. What this grunt didn't notice, and we didn't either until we were watching his body dissolve, was that only a short distance away there was a more stable vegetation breach that the rest of the grunts from J Division were now streaming over. It beat the prospect of body hopping.

I almost didn't go that night. My brother-in-law had nearly convinced me that I could join him in his enterprise. He had grown fat on DT pickings.

He said it was safe, and that apart from the occasional brother who stayed out too long, there was no copper, no traps, and the stuff was good and nutritious. It wasn't in the same place each day, but there seemed to be plenty of it around. It's just that when you grow up with Q Division as your career goal, it's just too hard to knuckle down to DT pickings, although I knew guys, good guys, who had given up the force for the easier life. At least it meant that you didn't have to give into the every whim of the Commander, and his whims were getting more strange and demanding by the week: "Fragaria with Red Stele Root Rot, if you please, Sergeant," was the latest.

DT's were not on my mind now though as I headed through the gap following the tracks of J Division. The rest of the guys followed me.

It was supposed to be an easy mission. Take and taste what we wanted, and bring a fragaria back to base for the Commander and his hermaphroditic harem. I'd done it before, but I wasn't really into it that night, and maybe that's what saved me.

I hadn't moved as fast as usual, but I had kept in

the shadows. I rounded the corner of a clump of tall grass and found a sight which keeps me awake at nights even now. All the guys of J Division were going down, slowly, silently, and almost painlessly, and by morning they would be oozing their guts onto the pine-needle covered soil. They must have been downwind. They say it's hard to resist once you get the smell in your nostrils. I wondered why it hadn't happened to me, but maybe that cold I'd picked up last time was in Cabbageville had blocked my nose.

Whatever it was, I couldn't smell a thing, but I needed to keep the rest of my division away from there and moving on to the target. I blocked the way and told my guys to take a different route as they came past me. I guess that one or two maybe caught the hint of beer on the wind, because I saw their eyes glaze over for a second, and nearly break line, but when they saw me blocking their way, they got back in step pretty quickly.

I wish I'd gone first. I should have. I guess I saved them from the beer, but I couldn't save them from the bait, and by the time I caught up with them it was too late. I held a dying teenage private and told him it was okay, he'd done good, and the Commander and his family would be proud of him. I didn't tell him that all his buddies had gone down with him, and that if only I had been at the front, not the back, maybe he'd still be alive.

Who were these people anyway? Copper, beer and then bait. How good did you have to be around here? It was then that I realized that I was the only one left. It's a lonely, scary feeling.

I got the fragaria and made it back with the first rays of sunlight chasing me across the yard. The vegetation breach blew away just as I crossed back over. I wondered if that had been placed just to trap those guys. I guess I'll never know.

I handed the Commander the fragaria, although why he didn't call it a strawberry like everyone else I don't know, or at least I threw it down at his foot. Let him pick it up, the SOB, and there and then I resigned; told them what I thought of the job and what I thought of him. Hoped he'd be apophallated by one of his harem as he was estivating—he didn't like that. Two divisions gone and he didn't even raise a hand, or give me a nod to acknowledge what we had gone through. It would have been hard for a fat slug like him to do that, but at least he could have tried.

I had thought about joining my brother-in-law in the DTs—but Dog Turds have never been my favorite delicacy—and I just couldn't do it. It was too ingrained in me to be someone better, so I headed back to the hills. I hopped a freight to Belfair, took the ferry up the Skokomish, and headed back into the woods.

They took me back. Sure, I'm a runt compared with some of my cousins here, but I still do my share, and in the evenings we'll sit around a rotting Chanterelle and I tell them about my life in Q Division in the city. I don't think they always believe me, and now sometimes I'd wonder about that too, but the nightmares still come back. It was real all right. Too real.

Ario Limax, Sergeant (Retired),
BS (Banana Slug) SWAT Team, Q Division

Glossary

apophallate: The process of separation after mating in which one slug will gnaw off its own or its partner's sex organ.

Ario Limax: Scientific name for the Banana Slug.

estivate: To become dormant during the summer.

fragaria: Genus name for strawberry.

hermaphrodite: Individual who has reproductive organs of both sexes.

red stele root rot: Common strawberry disease.

True Slime Tales #37

The Continuing Adventures of
Woodrow Cutter, TI
(Thaumaturgical Investigator)
Janice Clark

She undulated into my office, leaving a trail of slime that gleamed like the pearls around her lovely throat. She was dressed in red, a coy little number with a hood that nearly concealed her tentacles, but the plunging neckline and slit skirt left little else to the imagination. A tantalizing tendril of scent reached out to cloud my already beer-fogged brain. Jasmine with something musky. When she dipped an eyestalk at me, I nearly swallowed my cigar.

"Woodrow?" she panted, in a breathless voice that sent shivers down my back. "Woodrow Cutter?" Her whole body was quivering like a flamenco dancer.

"That's the name on the door, sister." Mesmerized by the luscious moistness of the pulsating mantle before me, I took my foot off the desk and tried to look nonchalant as I put out the cigar in my coffee cup and swept the empty beer bottles into an open drawer. "What can I do for you, gorgeous?" She was the most beautiful slug I had ever seen, and she was making goo-goo eyes at me.

"For starters, you might offer me a chair. The elevator's out and I just climbed seven flights of stairs."

I felt myself go pink from my foot to the base of my feelers. The office was in its usual condition, with grimoires and alchemical paraphernalia covering every available surface. Mumbling some inane excuse about the cleaning lady being on vacation, I hastily removed *Ten EZ Spells for Gastropods* and a couple of crucibles from the sofa. "Make yourself comfortable. May I offer you some refreshment? Beer? Comfrey tea?"

"Lemonade would be lovely, if you have it." She fluttered her eyestalks.

I could do lemonade. I'd mastered it in lesson three of my wizard's correspondence course. I slipped out my wand and murmured the appropriate words. Two sparkling glasses of lemonade appeared, complete with ice. As I handed her a glass, I put on a self-deprecating smile, prepared to respond with some humble disclaimer when she admired my skill, but she took it with only a polite, "Thank you."

Annoyed at her unenthusiastic response, and even more irritated with myself for craving approval, I growled, "Okay lady. What's an obviously classy dame like yourself doing slumming in my neck of the woods?" I took a sip from my own glass. It was sour.

"My name is Rosamonde DeHoode. My friends call me Rosie. I came to you because . . . because. . . . Oh, Mr. Cutter, I do so desperately need your help. My poor old granny has disappeared and I fear for her life." She ducked down, squinching up her eyestalks, and started quivering again.

"But why me? Why not go to the police? Wait a minute. DeHoode. Not DeHoode Amalgamated Farms, DeHoode's Confections, Hoode's restaurant chain. . . ."

She sipped her lemonade and shuddered. "I see you've heard of the family businesses. Granny is the majority stockholder and chairman of the board of DeHoode Enterprises. So of course you understand why I can't go to the police, why this matter must be handled with the utmost discretion. News of Granny's disappearance could rock the financial world as well as having social repercussions. We'd be hounded by *paparazzi*, our stock values could plummet, and worst of all, Granny might be in even greater danger. You must find her for me, Mr. Cutter."

She fluttered her eyestalks again. "My friend, Bonita Peepe, tells me you handled a sensitive matter for her last year, without attracting the attention of the press or the authorities. Bo says you're very talented as well as the soul of discretion."

I remembered the Peepe case. That flock of missing wooly bear caterpillars. I *had* handled that one rather well, I thought. Sort of. Well, it had all worked out in the end. They'd come home, anyway. Maybe Ms. Peepe hadn't told her friend all the details. I sat back in my chair and lit up another cigar. "Okay, Ms. DeHoode. I'm listening. Fill me in."

She elongated herself, shifting to a more comfortable position on the sofa. My feelers tingled as the side slits in her skirt revealed even more of her creamy tan mantle. "Call me Rosie."

My throat was dry. I took another swallow of the sour lemonade and almost choked. "Go on then . . . Rosie."

"Two days ago, I went to visit Granny at The Cottage. That's Grandpa's old hunting lodge in the woods. She spends most of her time there now, with only a few dozen servants for company. I took her a basket of goodies: some of our newest confections, nested in marigolds and wheat grass. We had a pleasant dinner, watched a little TV, and Granny went to bed early. The next morning, I was slithering through the gardens having a little nibble, when the housekeeper came looking for me. Granny hadn't come down to breakfast. They had knocked at her door, but there was no response." She smothered a sob, her feelers twitching with emotion.

Something about the basket she mentioned was setting off alarm bells in the back of my head. Something I'd heard recently—it was hard to concentrate with a gorgeous dame crying on my sofa. I'd think about it later. "Go on," I said. "What happened next?"

"I went up to her room and knocked on the door and called to her, but heard nothing. The door was locked. The housekeeper produced a key, and we went in, fearful of what we might find. We found . . . nothing. She was gone. Oh, Mr. Hunter, tell me you'll take the case. Tell me you'll find Granny. I don't know where else to turn." She averted her eyestalks again.

I knew in my feelers she was nothing but trouble, but, what the heck, I've always been a sucker for a beautiful dame in distress. "I'll do my best, Rosie" I heard myself saying. "I charge a head of cabbage a day plus expenses, and you'll also have to level with me. I need to know *everything*. What is it you haven't told me?"

She sighed. "I might have known I couldn't keep anything from *you*. It's my cousin, Wolfgang DeHoode. Wolfy and I are Granny's only living relatives, the sole heirs to DeHoode Enterprises. Our parents were killed in a horrible auto accident a few years back. Perhaps you heard about it?"

I shuddered. I remembered all right. The

headlines were splashed across all the papers, just like her parents had been splashed all over the highway. A carload of wealthy young slugs out on the town, too much champagne, a close encounter between their convertible and a salt truck. . . . It hadn't been pretty. So they'd had young ones. "Yeah," I said, feeling a little nauseous. "I heard about it. So it's just you and Wolfgang now?"

"Yes," she said, with a catch in her voice. "Wolfgang virtually runs DeHoode Enterprises since Grandpa died. Granny's semi-retired but still puts a tentacle in now and then. I used to help out a bit with the books, but lately Wolfgang prefers to keep it all to himself. There are rumors. . . ." She hesitated, turning her head away as if embarrassed. "I still keep in touch with some of the staff. Georgie . . . Mr. Porgie, the chief chemist at the candy factory, tells me there are rumors that Wolfgang has huge gambling debts, that he might be . . . 'borrowing' from company funds."

I nodded. "You think your cousin is tapping the till to support his gambling habit, and had to get Granny out of the way before she caught on."

She turned to face me again. "You're right, he could just be afraid of getting caught, but I'm also thinking he may have kidnapped Granny hoping to persuade her to change her will. That would leave me out in the cold, but that's not the important thing. I have a little money put away for a rainy day, and I can always sell my jewels. I'm just so afraid. . . . " She shuddered. "If he does get her to change the will, leaving him the sole heir, he might decide to go a step further and not wait for nature to take its course. Please, Mr. Cutter . . . Woody, we must find Granny before it's too late." She broke down in sobs.

I slithered over to her and patted her gently with my right tentacle. "There, there. Crying won't help. If we're going to rescue Granny, we'd better get going." I began throwing a few items in my backpack. "I'll need to see the scene of the crime for starters."

"I hope," she said, "that there's a better way out of here than the way I came in. I hate to think of going down all those stairs."

"No problem." I have a nifty little traveling spell (correspondence lesson number 12) that I use for emergency exits. In moments we were sliding down a giant beanstalk that had suddenly appeared outside my window. I think she would have been more impressed if it hadn't popped out of existence a couple of inches above the sidewalk, but it wasn't too far to fall and she refrained from commenting. A classy lady.

It was a long ride in her limo to The Cottage. I must have dozed off at one point, because I remember going over the river and through the woods, and then suddenly we were pulling into the circular driveway of this mansion that was maybe a little smaller than

Buckingham Palace. A prim-looking lady in black came out to meet us, followed by a bevy of pretty young things in little frilly maid's uniforms.

Rosie introduced me to Mrs. O'Grundy, the housekeeper, who gave me a sour look that told me I was as welcome as an invasion of mildew. We followed her upstairs to a third-floor room; she unlocked the door. She had enough keys on the ring to start her own scrap metal business.

"Nothing has been touched, as you requested." She spoke directly to Rosie, pointedly ignoring me, although she glanced my way now and then, probably to make sure I didn't steal the wallpaper.

"Thanks," I said, pushing my way through before Rosie could enter. The room was small, and reeked of lavender. Two small, high windows let in light but didn't look like anyone could get in or out. "Give me a few minutes to look things over. Oh, and I'll need slime samples from everyone who's been in the room in the last few days."

Mrs. O'Grundy looked more offended than before, if that's possible. Even Rosie stiffened a bit. "Really, Mr. Cutter. Surely you don't suspect myself or any of the staff. . . ."

We were back to formal again. "Ms. DeHoode," I explained as patiently as I could, "There are overlapping slime trails here. I need to rule out the legitimate ones so I know which, if any, don't belong."

I slid to the old lady's four-poster loam bed, took some vials out of my pack, and scooped up a trace of dried slime. Storing a sample for later use, I mixed a pinch with slime-trace powder and used my wand to spread it around. Faint traces glowed all over the room, but a line of hot pink ran like a neon sign from the door to the easy chair, with splashes on the little table beside it, and then to the bed. Granny hadn't left the room on her own foot.

I carefully backtracked on my own trail so as not to cover any clues. "Now, ladies, if you would be so kind. . . ."

Rosie let me take a smidge of slime off her foot. Mrs. O'Grundy reluctantly followed suit, as did the upstairs maids, Nanette and Babette. I color coded each sample, including my own, mixed it all with more tracing powder, and dusted the room again.

The room lit up for an instant with day-glo colors everywhere. Rosie's chartreuse led from the door to the little table and back, with heavy splashes on the basket sitting on the table. Mrs. Grundy and the maids showed up as faded pastels all over the room. My own orange ran straight to the bed and back. I barely glimpsed a double trail of electric blue—the unknown intruders—that ran from a behind a decorative screen to the bed and disappeared behind the screen again.

Then Rosie sneezed and stumbled against me, her feelers brushing my eyestalks. My wand flew up in the air, shooting sparks like a roman candle. Babette and Nanette screamed. Mrs. O'Grundy said something distinctly unladylike. By the time the wand stopped sputtering and I was able to focus again, the room looked like an explosion in a paint factory. Rosie and the others had a 60s tie-dye look and a glance downward told me I could use a visit to the neighborhood dry-cleaner myself.

Mrs. O'Grundy rounded up the hysterical maids and headed downstairs. "We shall be in the kitchen if you need us, *madame*. Please let me know when you and the *gentleman* are finished." She subsided into muttering something about having to have the whole place vinegared.

"I'm so sorry, Woody." Rosie was back to being friendly, flirty eyestalks and all. "I hope I didn't make you miss anything important."

"No problem, doll," I said, as I picked myself up and brushed traces of colored dust out of my eyes. "I saw enough." I pushed the screen aside to reveal a small door. A dumbwaiter. Of course. I opened the door, pulled up the platform, and scraped up some uncontaminated samples. "There were two of them, at least. Could be hired muscle with no slime records, but you never know. Let's check out the other end of this thing."

Before leaving, I took a closer look at the basket on the table. That would be the basket of goodies Rosie had mentioned. Nothing suspicious—slightly nibbled wheat grass and marigolds, an assortment of DeHoode confections, and a couple of foil wrappers with a few crumbs clinging. I took a sniff. Hosta and honey, with overtones of something I couldn't quite place. I bagged up the wrappers and picked up the basket as well.

The little alarm in my head was going off again. My buddy Clancy, on the narcotics squad, had been talking about some new street drug—Rhapsody, I think it was called. Every time they thought they had the goods on a pusher, he turned out to be carrying a harmless basket full of candy and wheat grass.

Rosie glanced back; she was already halfway to the stairs. "Why are you messing around with that basket? I told you I brought it myself. There's no clues there."

"Clues could be anywhere, sweetheart. Granny must have been sleeping pretty soundly to be carried away quietly with no signs of a struggle. She may have been drugged. The basket could have been tampered with. Unless you were watching it every minute up to the time you left it on the table?"

Her face went through a whole range of emotions but settled on wide-eyed innocence. "Oh, Woody, is it possible that someone actually put something in that basket that helped them to kidnap Granny? But that would make it my fault. . . ." She pulled a scrap of lace out of a pocket and wiped her eyestalks.

I headed downstairs to the basement. My wand was shorted out, but I could at least take samples at the other end of the dumbwaiter.

The trail from the dumbwaiter lead to the basement door and across the lawn to the driveway. It wasn't much to go on, but I scraped up slime anyway. The gardener thought he'd seen a delivery van the morning of Granny's disappearance, but couldn't provide any details. We headed back to the city.

Rosie was sniffling on the way back. "Oh, Woody, what do we do now? How are we going to find Granny?"

"Just let me stop off at the office to get a new wand and leave some of this stuff. I'll check it all out later. First, I'd like to get a slime sample from your cousin. Do you think you could arrange that?"

She brightened up so fast it was almost indecent. This whole caper was beginning to smell like month-old broccoli. We agreed she'd pick me up in an hour, and I returned to my office, which is also my apartment, to clean up. After running some quick tests on the contents of the basket, I conjured up a copy of it, stashing the original behind the secret panel where I keep my valuables and sealing it with my best protection spell. I was pretty sure someone would be showing up to retrieve the basket; I set the copy out in plain sight in the hope they wouldn't tear the place up searching. A quick call to my buddy Clancy, a couple of extra wands in my pocket in case Rosie had another sneezing fit, and I was as ready as I was going to be to invade DeHoode Enterprises.

Rosie had changed from the stained red outfit to slinky black. She may have been an amateur at the cloak-and-dagger business but she was giving it all she had. I still wasn't sure what her angle was, but I figured I might as well enjoy the game. I certainly wasn't going to tell her what I had seen before she knocked me over at Granny's house: A faint trace of chartreuse under the blue streaks, that told me Rosie had been in the room earlier, probably to unlatch the dumbwaiter door.

Rosie's driver parked the limo in the VIP section at DeHoode's Confections. We breezed past the guards, threaded our way between candy vats on the main floor, and slid up a ramp to the office area. Wolfgang's secretary saw us coming, through the large window overlooking the factory. "I'm sorry, Ms. DeHoode, but Mr. DeHoode is over in the QC lab. Could I help you with something?"

"It's okay, Sharla, don't bother to get up. I'm just picking up some papers Wolfy wanted. I know where they are. By the way, this is Mr. Cutter. He's helping us with some special work." We slid past the secretary's desk into the inner sanctum before she could get a word out.

I quickly took some scrapings from Wolfgang's chair. Rosie had something else in mind. She had pushed aside a portrait of old Armand DeHoode and was fiddling with a wall safe. She popped open the door and started shuffling through papers as if she knew exactly what she was after.

"Yes," she stage-whispered. "I knew it! Look, Woody."

I looked at the document she was unfolding. Interesting how she knew what it was before she opened it. It looked like a pretty amateurish forgery to me, but what do I know? Rosie was just closing up the safe again when the door to the office opened and in slid a pudgy slug wearing a white shirt and horn-rimmed glasses.

"Rosie? What are you doing in my office? And why is the safe open?"

Obviously Wolfgang was a little slow on the uptake. Rosie looked startled but immediately went on the offensive. "Don't act so innocent, Wolfy. We're on to your little scheme. Mr. Cutter and I have found the altered will, and we know you kidnapped Granny. Where is she?"

Wolfgang blinked a few times and shook his head, looking as confused as a chameleon on a chessboard. "What will? And what do you mean, where's Granny?

She called me this morning from a hotel in Bermuda. She says she has no idea how she got there, but she's having the time of her life. She sounded a little drunk to me."

That was what I wanted to hear. I whipped out my cell phone and quick-dialed Clancy. "The old dame's okay, Clancy. They stashed her outside the country, but she's reported in on her own. You and the boys can come on in."

Wolfgang looked more confused than ever. "Who's Clancy? For that matter, who are you? Rosie, what have you been up to now?"

A big guy in a white lab coat burst into the room. It was getting a bit crowded. I caught a glimpse of the newcomer's badge—G. Porgie. Must be Rosie's chemist friend. He glanced at the fake will on the desk. "Rosie, so you were right. We've caught you red-handed, DeHoode. There's enough evidence to put you away for life."

Obviously Georgie wasn't up on the script changes. All the puzzle pieces were falling into place, and it wasn't a pretty picture. I was willing to bet his slime trace would match one of the samples from Granny's room.

Rosie was frantically waving her feelers, trying to get him to shut up. She pulled a gun out of her handbag. "Georgie, darling, do be quiet. They're on to us. We've got to get away. My limo's outside. Let's go."

Sharla, the secretary, poked her head in the door. "Georgie, *darling*? Georgie, are you and Rosie. . . ? But you said you loved *me*." She burst into tears.

I could hear Clancy yelling. "Police. Everybody freeze. You with the basket, hold it right there." Rosie's hired goon must have finished searching my office; probably bringing in the supposed evidence. Nice timing. I caught a glimpse of something small flying through the air, followed by a splash.

Wolfgang was looking back and forth fast enough to get whiplash. "Please," he said. "Will someone tell me what's going on?"

Georgie zipped up to Rosie, grabbed her gun, and held it against her head. "Nobody make a move or Rosie gets a dose of salt pellets." Through the open office doors, I could see the cops had nabbed a guard, who was probably number two of the mystery slime trail at The Cottage. My facsimile of the goody basket was sinking into a vat of candy on the floor below. Georgie, with Rosie in tow, backed up to the railing overlooking the candy vat. "Back off, coppers," he yelled. "Me and the lady are going to leave here quietly, and you're going to stay out of my way." I pulled a wand, but was afraid of hitting Rosie. I'm still a little shaky on disarming an opponent without blasting bystanders; that's covered in the advanced course.

Georgie snarled at Rosie. "I told you we should

just salt him and be done with it. The old lady, too. But no-o-o, you had to get cute with your elaborate little scheme to get them both out of the way."

Rosie was sniffling. "I told you, Georgie. I couldn't kill them. Not even for you. They're all the family I have."

"You can run," growled Clancy, "but you can't hide. You're going down for manufacturing and distribution, punk. Not to mention drugging and kidnapping the old lady. Murder could get you the salt pit. Better quit while you're ahead."

Wolfgang still looked confused, but he got a crazy look in his eyes. "Leave her alone," he yelled. Whatever she's done, she's still family." I've never seen a slug move so fast. He knocked Rosie out of the way and was all over Georgie, both of them struggling to get control of the gun. Next thing I knew, Georgie was over the railing and following the basket into the candy vat.

Rosie screamed. "Georgie!" She zipped up to the railing. I couldn't be sure whether she dived, fell accidentally, or tripped over Sharla's foot, but she made almost as big a splash as Georgie did. It was all over in a moment. There was nothing to see but a few bubbles rising to the surface of the tankful of Hosta and Honey.

I looked away, feeling nauseous. Wolfgang had turned a sickly gray. Even Clancy looked a little shaken. Sharla stood looking over the railing, crying quietly.

The guard was still struggling to get away from the police. "Let me go. I didn't do nothing. Anyway, you've got no evidence."

Clancy looked at me. "What've you got, Woody?"

"Slime samples from the scene of the kidnapping, for starters. The real basket of drugged candy—the one he tossed was just a decoy. Probably slime prints all over my office, too. I hope he didn't do too much damage. There should be enough to put him away for keeps, unless the DA cuts him a deal for spilling his guts. If he has any sense, he'll clue you in on the whole drug operation. Better behind bars than in the vat, buddy."

Clancy slapped me on the back. "I owe you a beer for this one, Woody. The whole department has been trying to get a line on this Rhapsody junk for months, but every time we think we've got the goods on a pusher, he turns out to be carrying something harmless, like wheat grass."

"That's the secret," I said. "DeHoode's Hosta and Honey with a little added flavoring, and wheat grass laced with malt and yeast. Two perfectly harmless treats, but if you eat them together, you're off in la-la land. Too much and you'll never wake up." I turned to Wolfgang, who was still looking stunned. "The stuff's pretty addictive. You'd better get Granny home and into rehab, and make sure she doesn't have any stashed."

Wolfgang was finally starting to get it. "Are you saying that Georgie and Rosie have been manufacturing illegal drugs in *my candy factory*?"

Clancy nodded. "You got it, pal. I'm afraid we'll have to shut you down for a week or two while the boys check everything out, but as long as you cooperate, I don't think the DA will be pressing charges. I wouldn't try to leave town for a while if I were you. You can send someone else to bring your grandmother home."

"Well," I said, "I guess I'll go see how much damage was done to my office. Mr. DeHoode, I'll be sending you my bill, since you're Rosie's next of kin. Clancy, you can send one of the boys around to pick up the basket and other evidence. I'll catch you later for that beer."

I left to find a taxi. It's a lonely life, being a TI, but I felt that today I'd made the world just a little cleaner. Too bad Rosie turned out to be so rotten. She sure had been one beautiful slug.

SpikeSlug vs. 76 Octo

Maxwell Kier DiMarco

Once upon a time there was an octopus who was afraid of everything. He was afraid of fish. He was afraid of boats. He was afraid of sharks. He was afraid of sunken ships. He was afraid of everything in the world except his own tentacles. He thought he would explode from fear but he didn't. Instead he grew strong and turned evil and very bad. His tentacle tops became bombs in the shape of monster heads. His name was 76 Octo.

76 Octo climbed out of the sea and onto the beach. Then he climbed off the beach and into the city. He was going to explode the city with his new bombs because he was so selfish.

Meanwhile, in a tall building downtown, SpikeSlug was playing checkers with his friend, Baby Squirrel. SpikeSlug is a slug with two spikes on the top of the

shell he wears as armor. He was born a superhero with the power to be brave and strong. He believes in goodness and friendship power. If someone is in danger and wants to call him on a cell phone, just dial 600-0033!

Suddenly, a T-rex head shaped bomb exploded near by and the tall building shook a little. The checkers bounced from one square to another square and Baby Squirrel's chair fell down.

"Be careful, my friend," said SpikeSlug. "Or you may get hurt." SpikeSlug went to the window to see what was going on. Because he was up high, he could see nothing but clouds. "How will I be able to see through all these clouds?"

Without waiting any more, SpikeSlug jumped out the window and fell six hundred feet to the ground. He landed with a thud, upside down, right on his spikes! SpikeSlug got up and heard a strange voice.

"I wouldn't do that, if I were you."

SpikeSlug spun around to see who was behind him. There stood 76 Octo.

The fight began!

76 Octo threw a bomb shaped like a Venus Fly Trap head. SpikeSlug dove to the left to avoid it. Then 76 Octo threw a bomb shaped like a robot head. SpikeSlug dove to the right. Then SpikeSlug jumped out of the road and landed right on 76 Octo's head!

76 Octo began to smoosh into a slime puddle and his bombs exploded.

BOOM! BOOM! BOOM! BOOM!

The fight was over.

SpikeSlug went back to his game of checkers with Baby Squirrel. He did not see the slime puddle rolling into a ball and returning to the sea. . . .

Coming to a Logical Occlusion

John Dimes

N atalie, I decided to take an extended lunch break." Jacob Entemann grinned wickedly, his phone pressed between his shoulder and ear. He was rifling through a manuscript entitled "Memories From an Arid Clime." He hated the title almost immediately and decided that he hated the entire thing, unread. Changing his mind, he began skimming the few paragraphs. He wanted to be well informed as to why he hated the thing, while hating it nonetheless.

Entemann was the founder and editor for one of the most important magazines in the country, *The Cerebellineum, For This Century's New Minds*. Profitable, entertaining, informative. Thick as a phone book. Glossy. It was the "go to" magazine for whatever political climate existed, or for whatever celebrity type wished to voice an opinion, for all that it was worth. And it was well worth it.

"Yes, I'll be back Monday. Ha-HA! Yes, I'm in the country! However did you guess?"

It was well known that the handsome, fifty-two year old Entemann often took his extended lunches on Fridays, directly after his dry martini and Cobb salad (with extra "onion straws") lunches. As disciplined as Entemann believed himself to be, even he was alarmed at how out of control his martini and Cobb salad (with extra "onion straws") lunches had become. So out of control that the salads appeared to be a not so clever distraction from himself—or for those who would recognize—that he was indeed downing every glass that was constantly pushed at him at nigh imperceptible intervals.

Another dead give away at his state of drunkenness over his embarrassment: His face would inevitably be a sanguine, bee-sting red. "The week was hell, dear. You know it? Of course you do. Decided that I'd edit a few things here. Maybe plug away at the book?" Entemann suddenly looked hurt. "What book? The one I've been working on for two years now!"

It was known that Entemann's novel was a thing in progress for several more years than just two, yet it had still to emerge upon the world in its entirety. Like Truman Capote between the successful rock of *In Cold Blood*, and the hard place during the crafting of

Answered Prayers, he seemed desperate for some kind of spiritual support, some type of daily affirmation of his talents and abilities by liberally dropping chapter names—but no actual chapters—like: "Coming To A Logical Occlusion," or "For The Sake of Trembling Stabilities."

Again the appropriate "Oooh's" and "Ahh's" failed to encourage the book into any viable incarnate state. Into any current reality. All Entemann had to his credit was a well regarded two paragraph editorial piece, and an essay entitled "Coerced Into Christ: The Changing Moral Fiber of America" in issue #1 of *Cerebellineum*. After that, there was not another article or essay written by him since the magazine's inception.

Well, he'd written words, but it was across those of other writers.

"Brad Allen?" he started corrosively, then sighed. "Wants to tender another piece, huh? Well, send it along. I love his work. It's like traversing a rather ponderous, no—no *complicated* crossword, or—or you know those theme games, the—the find the words in the bunch games? I . . . I dunno what they're called right this minute. You know, where you have to find, um, *dog* or *Fido* or *Rin Tin Tin* spelled backwards and diagonally? Yes, huh-HA, yes that's it. That's what his work is like. Every odd word somehow stands out in that rich, uh, maelstrom he puts together. Four paragraphs alone are worth about five hours of serious reflection . . . *and re-writes* . . . ."

Many of the freelance writers involved with the *Cerebellineum* magazine had garnered more than their fair share of awards and accolades, those on staff however never really felt they themselves had any actual talent. Though heartily encouraged by Entemann, he discouraged them in a way that could only be described as "deceptively mirage-like."

He edited every article that came by him, and it was imbued with his own personal style. That is to say, his style greedily consumed all that it touched, leaving nothing of the original voice or paragraph but a frail, brittle husk of its former self. Writers would dread receiving edited copy from Entemann, however non-confrontational, or constructive the editorial hatcheting. Everything was soundly inscribed and informed by the *Chicago Manual of Style*, after all, and by Entemann's own brand of *lucid correctoria*. Every red stroke was a callously—yet, well intended—wound inflicted upon the very soul and psyche.

"Right, then," Entemann moved to the fridge for a cold, sweaty bottle of imported Hefe-Wiezen. "I won't be checking messages from here. Be kind to do that for me over the weekend. Anything important just call me. Otherwise, my dear, have a nice one. Bye bye!"

He sat his cellular on the small kitchen island, reached for a lemon. Sliced a wedge and dutifully tossed it in the glass.

A year ago, Entemann had taken over his grandmother's small, two story country house. From his estimation of things, he'd turned it from the gingham cluttered nightmare he remembered it to be as a boy, into a tiny country "estate" filled with stainless steel kitchen appliances, "meaningful" art pieces, and attractive leather sectional sofas and chairs stained a sober umber.

Along with the refitting of the house, there was the garden. He contracted an expert landscaper to put in an assortment of "highly recommended" garden pieces. "Now this here Nadina," Entemann remembered the salesman saying about a particular bush with little red berries, "don't need much water. And birds, you like birds? Well, they come at it! Come at it! And butterflies? Well we got all sorts-a stuff here that attracts them like mad! *Asclepias Tuberosa. Lantana*, and this here burgundy one, *Salvia Greggii* . . . ."

Everything was acceptable to Entemann, and no expense could be spared, to some degree. As long as there were roses to be had in the morning, and a hedge of honey suckles bushes to be had in the afternoons when it got hot. He'd loved sipping on the nectar from the thin pistils of flowers as a child. At some point, he wanted to revisit that summertime activity. Entemann sipped at his beer and smiled as he looked at the garden through the kitchen window.

Though he cherished his garden, he was not himself actually a gardener. His experience with potting shears and peat moss was minimal. He cultivated a few herbs and wild flowers from his apartment terrace back in the city. He reflected on the meager green square pot filled with its pitiful assortment of rosemary sprigs, and beleaguered roadside myrtle. No, the major gardening work was done by a rotating staff of experts provided by The Hudson Formist Company. Usually it was Crystal, the attractive grad school blond, with the dazzling "ice blues" who'd trotted in like a prized foal, wonderfully overwhelming her environment with cheer.

Or it was Chavers.

Now, Chavers was quite an enigma. Chavers was a strapping "brother" with an unusual accent. Mind you, Chavers was not one for talking. He was strictly business: Get the gardening done. Get to the next job. But when the man was occasionally persuaded into conversation, Entemann wasn't sure if his manner of speech was influenced by the south or by the streets. Regardless, it made Entemann retreat to quiet, pleasant places in his mind . . . if not in body.

Entemann went out the back door onto the small terrace and was immediately caught in the wave of grass- and jasmine-scented air. It was so intoxicating, he thought he might fall backwards. It was either that or the Hefe-Wiezen that made his head twirl like a majorette's tasseled baton. He slipped off his sandals and allowed the raw touch of grass to crunch and give beneath his weight. Suddenly he was a country boy, a Jethro Bodean. Sure, there was a small dot of a Monopoly piece-sized house set off in the distance momentarily disturbing his total ownership of the world, but if he continued on past a tree or two as he now did, it would be all his again simply by way of illusion.

He sat in the gazebo and drank his beer. He took in the scenery and suddenly remembered the manuscript he left on the counter. *I was going to read that*, he thought as he sipped away, letting the world fit him as if he were a piece of itself missing and returned to it at last.

Entemann woke in the dark on his side on the cushioned seat of his gazebo. He was surprised that he had fallen asleep at all. He wasn't a light weight, after all. He must've actually needed the rest. He swept his legs over the seat and onto the floor. He heard the intense sounds of the night time air. He was accustomed to the few crickets that managed to make themselves known over the usual din of the city, but out here, crickets and frogs ranted on unchallenged! He wondered what on earth they all could be communicating to each other that they haven't already discussed a thousand times before.

He looked up at the stars, clustered and shimmering. So close to the earth as to make one think they could be touched. The moon was just a sliver of copper rust toppled slightly to its side.

"Magnificent," he said as he blindly reached for his glass. He took a sip, and the lemon wedge bounced against his lips.

"Beautiful." He stretched his feet out across the gazebo floor. He stirred the dust a bit. Looking down, he saw the shimmer of a silvery lattice work raggedly crisscrossing the floor. Trails that stopped mysterious around a circular stain on the floor.

Entemann looked down in his glass: There were about four thumb sized presences bobbing about. Slugs, apparently. . . drowning slowly.

"Jesus!" he shrieked hurling the glass away. Frantically he spat and wiped at his face.

He was ready to leave the gazebo, then it hit him: *What if there were more?*

Looking out over the yard, he imagined he saw small shapes stirring in the grass. Moonlight catching intermittent movements that writhed and glistened. Where were his sandals?

"Oh, god. Oh, god." They were just at the edge of the yard where he left them in a fit of nature loving.

Entemann broke out in a cold sweat just thinking about it. How far was his house, he wondered? It really wasn't that far. Couple of trees and a bound away. Nothing too terrible. Easy going. Still, he wanted to be all spirit right now. Out of the body, sailing away from the moment.

A childhood memory of a camping trip blindsided him: A great camping trip with his brother and father—hiking, pitching tents, campfires, fried fish. And poison ivy. Oh, how he laughed at his older brother when he accidentally blundered into a patch of wild ivy mixed with sumac. Entemann remembered how he teased his brother mercilessly. He also remembered his own comeuppance. His brother put a huge banana slug in his sleeping bag. He remembered the warmth and the weight of the thing. So nearly imperceptible was its touch that his reflex, his reaction to it, was nil. Only as the thin trail of mucous began to dry and cool at his throat did he recognize that there was something on him.

He recalled his brother's humorous, yet guilt tinged re-telling of the events, how he had waited outside of the tent for what seemed an age for Entemann's scream. How he had found Entemann wide-eyed, trapped in a cataleptic rigidity. What was it the doctor had called it? *Limaxaphobia?* A fear of slugs.

Entemann was once again threatened by the fear of that obscene touch, that warmth that was deceptively pleasant. A muscled, liquid thing, roving mindlessly across his flesh. Now, however, Entemann was closer to hysteria than to catalepsy. He checked his immediate surroundings for any more slugs, then curled up in the gazebo like a small frightened child. He knew that his sleep would be fitful, but from the little he understood about slugs, and snails for that matter, they were nocturnal creatures. With the morning would come renewed courage.

By nine o'clock the next morning, a bleary eyed Entemann was on the phone to The Hudson Formist Company.

"I need someone to come out today. Preferably a specialist on—um—slug maintenance? No. No, I don't want to *maintain* them. Actually, I want them gone you see, and—Yes. That's right. But—but—but—it is something, I tell you! Not since I was a child have I been so—oh, you'll send someone out? What time? Can he come sooner, I mean it's just awful."

Entemann paused, tensed. "Yes, I know I live far out! It's the country. Albemarle County, but I don't see why I should be penalized because—oh, oh, I understand. He's in Waynesboro right now. It'll . . . it'll take a while. I understand. Forgive me. I mean, I know how it sounds. They're just little things. Little things, but—fine, fine, I'll be expecting him them. Thank you. Much appreciated."

Two o'clock rolled around, and a tattered blue pick-up crunched across the gravel road. Entemann hurried to the door. Words tumbled out in an excited rush, "Please, please come in!"

Standing in the doorway was a dark haired, sienna-skinned man in his early forties.

"Mr. Entemann?" asked the soft-spoken man.

"Exactly. Out in the back—"

"Adrian San Mateo." He extended his hand.

Dumbfounded, Entemann looked down at the proffered hand. San Mateo merely smiled. An awkward moment for Entemann, an apparently not so awkward for San Mateo. Entemann shook his hand.

"What's the problem?" asked San Mateo.

"Um, slugs."

"Oh, right, right. Slugs. Let me go back to the car for my manifest, 'kay?"

Impatiently Entemann watched as the wiry little man went to his truck and rummaged through several tablets on the front seat. Entemann also noticed that he seemed to be talking to himself. No. He was talking to a cat. San Mateo was bringing said cat—a beautiful orange tabby—with him into the house.

"Uh, I'm allergic," explained Entemann.

"Not to Eurydice. No problems with dandruff. That's what people are actually allergic to. Dander, not the fur like most people think, see?"

"I . . . ."

"Let's go to the backyard, 'kay?"

It struck Entemann suddenly that San Mateo

resembled a young Sal Mineo, the actor who played the James Dean's ill-fated friend in *Rebel Without A Cause.*

"Backyard?"

"Yes. Where the slugs are?"

Oh, god. I'm staring, thought Entemann. "Right! Right, right. Right this way."

The one thing Entemann hated, other than being perceived as stupid, was being perceived as a *stereotype.* As a caricature of the desperate, calculating old queen. But here he was, inexorably drawn toward the man—like the moth to the quintessential flame—as he voyeuristically catalogued every step, every motion San Mateo made as he roved about the garden. And damned if the man didn't act like he owned the place! Smoothing the bark on a tree here, cupping a blossom laden limb in one hand, so to accept any and every aroma proffered there. Oh, and the worst part—if such a thing could actually be considered the worst part— San Mateo, casually untucked his shirt to blot the sweat from his forehead and face. For approximately 35.9 seconds, (an eternity looped on the reel of his mind), the lean, muscled torso of a Latino statue of David graced Entemann's backyard.

"Mr. Entemann?"

Damn! He was staring again. "Um, yes?"

"I've figured out what the problem is."

The problem, thought Entemann, *is that I haven't*

been with anyone in, what? five years, that I've been sublimating my desire by drinking myself into a quaintly entertaining stupor, that I've been throwing myself into the wall of my ridiculous magazine?

What he said was, "Um . . . and that would be?"

"Follow me," said San Mateo.

"Anywhere, Sal Mineo," he whispered, ruefully.

"What?"

"Nothing. Lead on, Mr. San Mateo."

"'Kay."

They strolled over to a hedge, and San Mateo directed Entemann's gaze to an area beneath the hedge clumped with mulch and freshly turned earth, the latter a result of Eurydice, San Mateo's cat.

"Why is your cat—?"

"Eurydice is a special cat, Mr. Entemann. I trained her to look for snails, slugs and their eggs."

"What?" he laughed. "You can actually train a cat to do that?"

"Sure you can. You can train 'em to do anything, just takes a little longer. Plus there's gotta be something in it for them," said San Mateo.

"Ugh! You couldn't possible mean, I mean you don't feed it—?"

"No, no! The mucous slugs produce makes it a hassle for animals to eat. Even for their natural predators, like frogs. Look."

They watched as Eurydice dug determinedly at

the earth with absolutely no results for what seemed like a long time. Just when Entemann thought he'd completely zone out, San Mateo shouted. "Eureka! Look there!"

Entemann's expression was stark as he stared down at the two fat slugs that had been churned up from the moist humus.

"Good girl! Good girl!"

"Yuh, yes. Good girl," said Entemann with detest.

"Now," said San Mateo, cheerfully, "I could let Eurydice pounce on 'em. Slugs hate fur, or hair. But watch this." San Mateo reached in his pocket and produced a small sandwich bag filled with a fine white powder. "Talcum," he pronounced.

The tiny creatures writhed terribly as the talc hit them and instantly drew all the moisture from their bodies. It was as though they were being squeezed by unseen fingers. Immediately Eurydice commenced to batting the dying things around.

"Ain't that like a cat? Buy 'em an expensive toy? *Nada.* Get 'em a cheap piece of string, and it's like, whoopie! Party time!"

"So it would appear." Entemann relaxed, reveling vicariously in the cat's crude entertainment.

"Looks like fried okra, huh?" laughed San Mateo.

"Umm . . . so, uh, what can we do about the slugs?" Entemann muttered, desperate for a change of subject.

"Well, you have stuff that keeps them away already, like lantana. But you also have stuff they really like, like delphinium," San Mateo said, pointing to a row of buttercups. "And these marigolds. Very attractive to a slug."

Entemann looked to the ground again, worried.

"Listen, I'm not gonna lay down a lot of unnecessary chemicals, or nothing. I don't think it requires that much attention. Besides, you saw how long it took Eurydice to dig around. I'm going to my truck. Get a few things. I'll lay down some cedar chips around the bases of all the bushes. Sprinkle some powdered ginger."

"Powdered ginger? Talc? All sounds like holistic medicine," said Entemann.

"Exactly. Exactly. Don't want to harm the earth any more than necessary, right?"

Entemann smiled.

"Didja happen to eat eggs this morning?" asked San Mateo.

"Uh, yes. I did, as a matter of fact."

"Donate the shells to the cause, that'll help make a sharp barrier against them."

Entemann instantly decided he'd crack the remaining eggsnuneatenn across everything. San Mateo made for the house, then suddenly spun on his heel.

"Say, Mr. Entemann, you got any beer?"

Entemann was alarmed. "Beer? Uh—if you're thirsty I have—"

"No, no. It's not for me. It's for the beer traps. For the slugs. They like beer, see? They drown in it and—"

"Oh, yes! Yes, I discovered that for myself last evening."

"I could use some water, though," said San Mateo. "Kinda hot out here."

"Yes, of course." Entemann inwardly congratulated himself for staying prurient thought free.

They went into the house, leaving Eurydice to her own devices, which was to torment the muck-encrusted bodies of the two dead slugs and roll around aimlessly in the grass.

In the shadow of a nearby hedge, a slug the size of a toddler's fist sat on a branch. It eyestalks were trained upon the cat. Slowly it ventured out along the branch, its slimy body shimmering with an eldritch light. The slug dripped thick, translucent streams of mucous down upon five motionless slugs waiting in the grass below, until they were caked in a bulbous spheres of jelly. The spheres enlarged—fed by the slug above and the five below—until the individual spheres finally impacted and merged into one perfect sphere. The moisture that pooled beneath the sphere was gradually absorbed into the earth.

Just then, the large slug fell from the branch.

Eurydice reacted to the sound and followed it toward the bushes. She spied the enormous slug lying dead on its back. Tentatively she approached the thing, sniffed at it, and, in the process, found herself stuck in some kind of sticky pool. It was as though she were caught in quicksand. The more she struggled, the more she was sucked in. Eurydice railed as the thick soup pulled her further into the dark, loose soil. In moments, she was sucked headlong into the earth and was gone.

San Mateo came around back of the house toting a tool box in one hand, and a beer can in another. He took a few pulls on the beer before he put it and the toolbox on the ground. From the toolbox he produced a bottle of Thai powdered ginger and a carton of Epsom salts. He also got out three beer traps made from the tops of one-liter bottles, which he placed strategically beneath the nearest bush. He poured the beer in the traps, then began to spread the cedar chips. After that, it was simply a matter of sprinkling the ginger and Epsom salts around the rest of the yard.

He snapped his fingers as he remembered the sandwich bag filled with crushed eggshells— painstakingly fished from Entemann's trash can—in his pants pocket. Any slugs who crawled across that, San Mateo thought, would cut themselves but good.

After about twenty-five minutes, Entemann came out to the terrace to see San Mateo's progress. He was kneeling beside the toolbox, putting things away. "Just finishing up, Mr. Entemann."

"Great. Great. I really can't thank you enough."

"You can always thank me enough," said San Mateo.

Entemann was about to say *How so?*, when San Mateo walked over and handed him his business card.

"Ah! Wonderful." Entemann inwardly blasted himself for forever translating the most innocent statements into such ridiculously self-serving double entendres. He vowed that at some point very, *very soon*, that he would populate his fantasies with a more obvious, and willing, participants. "I'll give you a call if anything changes."

"Great," San Mateo beamed. He began looking around the yard for the cat. "Eurydice," he called. "*Eurydice*! Come on girl!"

Entemann ventured out to the trees and the gazebo along the edge of his property to look for her while San Mateo went toward the bushes beside the house. He crouched down the ground. "Eurydice," he called to the shadows beneath the bush.

He saw something shift. Something wet. Gradually Eurydice emerged.

"Sweetheart! Hey, Mr. Entemann, I found her!"

When Eurydice emerged from the undergrowth, she was a terrible mess. Here fur was matted with some type of goo. She looked so bad, he almost didn't want to touch her.

"Baby, what's wrong?" he said, reaching out for her.

Eurydice cringed away, and skirted the edge of the yard as she streaked around to the front of the house.

Entemann arrived just as the cat sped past him. "What was that all about?"

"I dunno. She must've fell into something. Looked kinda sticky."

"Probably honey," said Entemann. "There's a lot of area to explore. I'm sure a bevy of angry bees is forgetting about her even as we speak." Then grimaced at the actual prospect of a bee or hornet infestation.

San Mateo didn't look entirely convinced. "Well, she's getting a bath when she gets home. Like it or no."

Evening crept up slowly as Entemann poured over various manuscripts, an act scored with the playful arpeggios of Astor Piazolla on his bandoneon and, later, by the somber bassoon-like tones of the duduk, played by Armenian artist Djivan Gasparyan. From time to time he would be attentive to a phrase or two from a melody, but in general he was so familiar with the music that his concentration rarely strayed from his work. More to the point, he was a kind of musical Tourette's case, erratically bursting into precognitive warbles as counterpoint to anticipated moments in the music. But eventually, he was distracted by some kind of hiss or squeal in the music that hadn't been there before. "What the hell is that?"

Entemann rose to check his stereo. He turned the volume up a notch to hear what the problem was, but that only drowned out the sound he'd heard. *Not the stereo*, he decided.

Something crashed in the kitchen. Irritably, he turned down the stereo, and ventured to the rear of the house. Oddly, the sound he mistook as stereo static grew louder as he neared the kitchen. Once he entered the kitchen, he saw a coffee can had fallen to the floor; its grounds had spilled everywhere.

"How in the world—?"

Though the static-like squeal was irritating, Entemann decided to clean up the mess first. Testily, he looked for his broom, but a piece of paper on the floor caught his eye. He removed it gingerly from the coffee grounds and shook it off.

There was something written on it. The penmanship, if one could call it that, was ragged, child-like and nearly incomprehensible. Also it seemed that it wasn't written with ink, but with the coffee grounds sprinkled across—what was it, glue? Resin? Some kind of viscous material that he couldn't figure.

He read the note:

Mother as father. Man as woman.
Gliding on slow silver. Never quick.

Patiently destiny awaits.
Destiny is destination.
We rain thick mire. Our soft glass drowns.
The slow earth is quickened.
Foes on silver paths. Lost forever.
Cleaved with shimmering scars.
Now, we his children.
His puzzled skin. I, We, Him.
Together. Parted. We come.
We, oh him, oh, Metztli. Come.
We come.

When Entemann finished the thing, he was torn. Utterly torn. Should he be afraid of the strange missive or should he edit the hell out of the damned thing! Before he could decide, the music stopped in the living room. He was immediately aware of the rise in the keening sound. It was coming from outside, this sound. Like the metallic whistling of a tea kettle, but more . . . *organic.*

He moved to the kitchen window, and saw beneath the cat's eye sliver of moonlight, the hideous forms as they twisted in the grass in his backyard. The ground was teeming with hundreds upon hundreds of slugs. It appeared that some were dead, but beneath the dead, living ones were fighting their way to the surface. He fancied he could actually detect the hiss of their viscous flesh as they slid across one another. That, and the thin sound of what he understood now to be their wailing voices.

Entemann, in a near panic, rooted for San Mateo's card. He grabbed his cell phone from the kitchen island. The phone chirped minutely in Entemann's ear for several moments. His heart sank when he thought the man's voice mail would kick in.

"San Mateo," a voice said, in lieu of "Hello."

"Oh, Mr. San Mateo! Thank goodness you answered!"

"Mr. Entemann? Is there a problem already?"

"I would say so!. Listen! Can you hear that unholy din?"

"I'm sorry?"

"Just a moment." Entemann pointed the phone in the direction of the yard, held it there for a moment. "Do you hear—?"

"What's that?"

"I don't know! Your slug remedy seems to have caused them quite a bit of distress."

"That's not right," said San Mateo, accompanied by a blurt of static.

"They are out there! Thousands of them. They're huge! I—I can't believe—oh!" Entemann, cried out, springing backward as a slug flung itself against the window.

"Mr. Entemann?"

"I don't expect they'll let me get at my car," Entemann said. "They left me a note. A note! 'He's, coming! He's coming!'"

"Who's coming? What are you—?"

"I don't know, what—? Metztli? Metztli. . . *oh my god!*"

"Mr. Entemann?! Mr. Entemann?!" San Mateo's thin voice spilled from the cell.

Entemann watched helplessly as the slugs began coiling, one upon the other in a circular mound at the center of the backyard. A thick foam of sticky mucous drenched them, shellacking them together as the slugs coalesced into familiar shapes: Arms, legs, torso, until they had become the rudimentary form of a man.

From his end of the line, San Mateo heard the clatter of the phone as dropped to the floor, followed by a series of muffled screams from Entemann.

San Mateo had been waiting along the gravel road near Entemann's house for nearly forty-five minutes before the Albemarle County police car arrived. He got out and flagged it down.

The brown cruiser pulled up. A thin officer stepped out. "You're the gentleman that called? Adrian San Mateo?"

"Yes, officer."

"You say that there was an intruder on the premises?"

"Yes, as I said to the dispatcher, Mr. Entemann called me very upset—scared. Then he dropped the cell phone—I . . . I heard screaming . . . "

The officer sized him up. "So, you haven't been inside at all?"

"Not since this afternoon." The officer stared. "He hired me to do some yardwork," San Mateo explained, defensively. "Can we just go up and see if he's okay?"

"Calm down, sir. You need to stay down here."

"But—Okay. Fine. I'll stay here."

The officer looked at the house. Lights were on upstairs and down, but from the road there was no discernible movement throughout. It was one-thirty in the morning.

Just then, San Mateo's cell phone rang. He fumbled for it. "*Mr. Entemann?* Are you—What?" The officer, who had only gone a few steps toward the house turned and looked at San Mateo. "There's an officer—At the bottom of the drive. Yes. I'm here, too."

The officer turned away and resumed his walk to the house. San Mateo, despite the officer's instructions, followed close behind.

"It's open!" a voice shouted from inside.

"Mr. Entemann?" the officer called. "What is your location?"

"Up here," Entemann replied, sleepily.

They found him in the bedroom, lying calmly and unabashedly naked amid tangled bedclothes.

"Sir," said the officer, obviously angry. "We got an emergency call from your friend here. He was under the impression that you were being confronted by an intruder."

"An intruder?" Entemann smiled.

The officer glared at San Mateo and Entemann in turns. "You were screaming. I thought you were being killed!" San Mateo practically shouted.

Entemann swung his legs lazily over the side of the bed and strolled to the closet. He took his time donning a silk robe. "I'm sorry, officer. But there seems to have been a misunderstanding. As you can see, I am in no danger. No danger at all." He settled himself on the bed again. "Have either of you ever heard of Metztli? Tecciztecatl?"

"Um, he's what—? Mayan? Aztec?" asked San Mateo.

"Aztec. Tecciztecatl was—is?—the moon god. Apparently he also has dominion over slugs and snails. Interestingly, he's sometimes called Coyolxauh-qui." He laughed. "Which is funny because Coyolxauh-qui is the female moon god."

San Mateo narrowed his eyes at Entemann. "And this is relevant because . . . ?"

"Was there or wasn't there an intruder this evening, sir?" the officer asked, evenly.

"There was," Entemann paused, searching for the right word, "a visitor," he answered. Returning to his story he said, "Legends about Tecciztecatl vary, but essentially the story goes that Tecciztecatl was supposed to be the sun god. But he feared the sun and was afraid sacrifice himself in fire in order to ensure that the sun would continue to shine on the Earth. So, that honor, if one can call it that, went to Nanauatzin instead. And, because he failed, Tecciztecatl, in the form of a rabbit, was thrown into the moon and charged with carrying it on his shoulders for all eternity."

Entemann paused, his listeners seemed both interested and annoyed. "But what people don't know is that the moon was never meant to be a punishment, but a mantle, passed on from generation to generation. It is, in essence, a sacred task. And name Tecciztecatl has become less of a name and more of a title. Like King or Queen." He paused again, "Or God."

"Where does Metztli fit into all this?" San Mateo asked. "On the phone you said 'Metztli. Metztli' just before you started screaming."

"On the last night of the waning moon—which just happens to be tonight—creatures in the moon god's—goddesses'?—domain can achieve a sort of sentience. And power.

"And?" asked San Mateo.

But Entemann didn't answer right away. He stared blankly at San Mateo and the officer remembering how the entity came into his home. By the time it arrived on the back porch, it had morphed from a collection of slimy, slithering, disgusting *slugs* into what could only be described as an amalgam of Entemann's ideal man. Except for one thing: The being's genitalia seemed to flux and all Entemann could discern was a wavering phantom penis juxtaposed with a spectral vagina.

Entemann spoke, his voice dreamy and far away. "'I am Metztli,'" he said. "'I am both male and female. My children are the third gender. The self- sustaining absolute. They embody the procreative powers of both male and female. As do I. And tonight, as the moon dies and is reborn, we celebrate our sacred duty, our devotion to Tecciztecatl, to Coyolxauhqui. We have chosen you to engage with us in the sacred dance—'"

"What the hell happened already?" snapped the officer.

Entemann paused a moment, flushing, as he remembered Metztli's words, whispered hotly against his ear: *"The moon is a sacred gift that must be passed on from generation to generation. From parent to offspring."* Entemann shook his head, then laughed. "It seems I'm going to be a father. . . ."

A Matter of Taste

Frederick J. Masterman

The wine—magnificent!

"The presentation—superb!

"The *taste*—ethereal!"

The server beamed. The guest was delighted. All was well.

Sidney Surient dreamily put another mouthful of his entrée upon his tongue, savoring the sensation, inhaling the odor, ecstatic over the taste. Heaven must have restaurants like this.

Across the table, his friend and colleague Stuart Pekkah shook his head in wonder. Even more so in disgust, as Sidney closed his eyes and gave an expression of gustatory orgasm.

"How can you do that?" Stuart asked.

"Do what?" Sidney asked, wide-eyed with feigned innocence.

"Eat—that—whatever it is?"

Sidney looked at his plate. In the sauce of garlic and butter, which exuded an aroma which he loved and Stuart did not, delicate slices of his entrée remained excitingly hot. The platter, itself a magnificent example of Thai artwork, rested over a warming flame. He inhaled deeply.

"Stuart, you are *so* limited. To think, I chose to bring you here, to my treasured restaurant, my gastronomic Shangri-La. I thought you'd appreciate it."

"I admire your mind, Sidney, but not your taste in restaurants."

Asian Extreme was the newest, and thus far the most popular of the restaurants in Imperial Beach, which graced the oceanfront overlooking the Pacific near San Diego. It was noted for its fascinating menu, and for skills unmatched in the preparation of exotic dishes.

"It takes some practice, I will grant you," Sidney said, sipping from his goblet of *Chenin Blanc*, the French wine which perfectly complimented his meal. "But it's an adventure, Stuart, the adventure of dining on the best the world has to offer."

Stuart begrudgingly nodded, and looked at his mundane dish of broiled burger and something that might have been green beans but prepared in a manner that disguised a specific origin. It was such an ordinary plate, but he had to admit that the flavor of the vegetable was remarkable, and the taste of the meat most pleasurable.

"Like your burger?" Sidney said, with a smile.

"The only normal thing on that bizarre menu," Stuart replied, trying another bite of his burger. "I'll have to say that this is very good."

"It ought to be, considering its source."

"Some wondrously fed cow, I'd guess. A burger is a burger, wherever served."

"Not quite. Actually it's a fine mixture of rat and kangaroo."

Stuart turned a shade of green and placed his fork on the table.

"What? Are you serious?"

"Most definitely."

"I think I'm going to be ill."

"Ridiculous. The roo and the rat are common-place food in some parts of the world, and as clean and healthy as any American cow—which may not be so healthy—madly diseased for all we know. And in this place," he gestured around the elegant dining room, "you know you are getting the absolute best."

Stuart sipped from his wine glass, a mundane California merlot.

"It may be healthy, and it does taste good, but I've lost my appetite. At least the vegetables are normal. Or appear so."

"Quite normal. A type of seaweed marinated in

ostrich blood and then sautéed to perfection."

"My god, Sidney! You are a sadist. Why did you bring me here anyway?"

"I wanted to introduce you to this restaurant, where you can get any—and I mean *any*—type of animal in the world, prepared and served in an excellent manner. Though you may have lost your taste for burger, I want you to sample a tiny, tiny bit of what I'm eating."

Stuart looked askance at the dish before Sidney. Long strips of white meat, slightly curled at the edges, simmered in the sauce.

"It looks like some type of whitefish. No doubt raised by insane islanders somewhere who eat it raw. At least you've had it cooked."

"Try it."

"I'd rather not."

"Come on," Sidney cajoled. "We've been friends for years. Maybe it was a mean trick to get you here and spring an exotic burger on you. I thought that once you tried it you'd be impressed. Anyway, one tiny bite of this."

Stuart slowly nodded. Sidney knew he was not adventurous. However, things change overnight with the right circumstances. He sliced a very small bit off one of the fillets and handed his fork to Stuart, who reluctantly took it.

"You owe me for this," Stuart said, and bravely

put it in his mouth, chewed and swallowed. "You know, I hate to admit it—but that's damned good. Sort of a shrimp consistency, and a wonderful flavor. Okay, out with it, what kind of fish?"

"No fish. Sea slug."

Stuart's eyes bugged again. "*Sea slug?*"

"Nudibranch. Wonderful, isn't it?"

"Sidney, you study those things, write books on those things, have made a bundle of money from experiments and research on those things. But *eat* them?"

"And why not? This dish is better than any loggerhead turtle or freshwater pike, no matter how well prepared." He selected another piece of the entrée, and closed his eyes with delight as he absorbed the flavor. "It's *Saussarelle D'Tochuina* and I've never tasted better."

"That's the Orange Peel Nudibranch, isn't it?" Stuart's field of expertise was the Phylum Brachiopoda, but he did have knowledge of other branches of marine life, such as Class Gastropoda, which included the nudibranchs.

"Correct, my friend. The only edible sea slug. To date."

"Sea slugs are notorious for the poison in their flesh, aren't they? Means of defense and all that? They're deadly to eat."

"As far as we know," Sidney said, finishing the

last morsel on the platter. "Even the orange peel was considered dangerous at one time. No more. I couldn't be happier."

Stuart picked up the menu, which Sidney asked the waiter to leave. The multitude of entrees was impressive. He glanced down the list more carefully, many names totally unfamiliar to him. He stopped, staring at one offering.

"Sidney, I know you mentioned loggerhead turtle, but I assumed you were joking." He lowered his voice. *"It's here, on this menu."*

"I know," Sidney replied with a conspiratorial wink. "Marvelous, isn't it? *Any* food in the world, here at our fingertips."

"It's an endangered species," Stuart said, his voice still low, his countenance grim. "What kind of restaurant is this?"

"Asian Extreme lives up to its name. There are actually several menus. One for ordinary guests. Others for special persons, as myself."

Stuart closed the menu. "I'm as dubious as you about some endangered species. Some ought to be endangered. Thwarting the natural course of evolution by protecting certain animals seems noble, but it's often misdirected, and impedes the natural course of events. But flaunt the laws? Not very smart, Sidney."

"The laws are not flaunted. Merely set aside. Quietly. If you wish a tiger steak, a king cobra fillet, pangolin fritters, or crocodile shish kebab, you don't have to travel to Thailand or China. You can get it here."

"Illegally."

"Oh, I guess you could say that. But Nontawat Srisai—he's the proprietor of Asian Extreme—is extremely careful. With the wonderful Asian population of California it was only natural that his type of restaurant would find its way to our shores. But it is not only the Asian palate that appreciates variety."

"How true," Stuart replied, "if you're any indication."

"Nontawat and I have become friends over the past year, since he opened this marvelous establishment. I'm even considering investing some money in it—his suggestion. It might be lucrative. And get me free dinners of the most supreme character." He chortled at this remark.

Stuart looked back at his plate, mostly untouched. Then he picked up knife and fork and gingerly tried another taste of the roo-rat burger. "You know, this isn't half bad, Sidney." He sampled more, and slowly nodded his head. "You might be right. I can see how a person could get intrigued by different flavors of food." He ate another mouthful.

"It's not only the flavors," Sidney replied, placing his napkin on the table. "It's the *source* of some of the dishes that intrigues me. Not the recipes but the animals themselves. Especially the nudibranchs, these wonderful sea slugs. Nontawat informed me that he has ordered a new type, bred purely for dining! Can you imagine that? I must taste them, perhaps next week."

"I can't promise I'll join you," Stuart said, finishing the last bite of the roo-rat burger. "This may be tasty, but it's the end of my eating adventures here." He looked intensely into Sidney's eyes. "Please, Sidney, be careful about getting too involved in the operation of this place. That illegal world of exotic animals, the endangered ones especially, can be dangerous for the people who get embroiled in it."

"Please, I've been at this a long time, and I've dined in eating establishments in the most bizarre places. This is one of the best. Believe me, Nontawat will do everything to protect one of his best customers, perhaps an eventual partner."

After a dessert of elegantly served pineapple and papaya, Sidney raised his huge frame from the table to leave.

"What about the check?" Stuart asked.

"Not to worry, my friend," Sidney said with a chuckle. "In places like this, there are no checks. All paid in advance, no visible exchange of money, an untraceable dinner. I told you it was safe. I have excellent taste in everything I undertake, from money to meals."

The creature was one of the most beautiful on earth, resplendent with a host of vibrant colors from its head to tail. Its body was yellow orange at the fringe, which faded to scarlet red, which faded again to darker purple at the crest of its back, where a branchial plume ran the length of its body—dozens of orange, red, and yellow-red hair-like appendages, the cerata. This array of tentacles stored algae stolen from coral for sugar production and stinging nematocysts stolen from anemones for protection. It slowly undulated across the base of the small tank, which simulated the ocean floor, gorging itself on whatever food lay in its path. It was a safe and predator-free environment for *Flabellina iodinea*, this watery home in Sidney Surient's laboratory at Pacific Research. Safe from predators. But not safe from Sidney Surient.

Nudibranch research. The study of the largest suborder of the exotic sea slug. It was a field little explored until Sidney Surient appeared on the scene.

Twenty five years before and fifty pounds slimmer, Sidney first amazed his doctoral thesis mentors at the University of California, with his imaginative experiments, studying various poisonous forms of sea life and the toxins they produced. Years with the Scripps Institute raised his reputation to new heights, where eventually his interests settled on the nudibranchs, the astounding world of the most colorful sea slugs on earth.

"A beautiful sight, don't you think, Cynthia?" Surient asked. "The procedure of selective breeding and enriched diet has worked. It's nearly four inches long, twice the size in the natural world."

Sidney took great pride in his skills of altering nature in the direction he chose. He found that the right diet could produce the most wondrous creations.

Cynthia Gorde sat on a lab stool next to Sidney. A doctoral candidate in her late twenties, she filled the lab coat with delightful curves which Sidney frequently enjoyed studying—when she wasn't looking.

And she was quite bright, even brilliant with her experiments. Of course Sidney gave her few compliments and rarely acknowledged her discoveries. Intending, as he had done for years with other graduate students, to file their work away and claim it as his own, properly disguised, at a later date.

"Do you actually believe *Flabellina* secretes toxins when threatened?" she asked.

"That, my dear, is what we are going to find out," Sidney replied.

"I appreciate your invitation to watch a phase of your work," she said. "It's a great opportunity to learn—"

"It is no trouble at all, Cynthia," he said, placing a fat hand on her shoulder and feeling her slightly cringe. Interesting, he thought, how creatures respond to negative stimulus.

"This research," he continued, removing his hand and turning back to the tank, "interests me in all its aspects, and I enjoy encouraging others, like you, to be imaginative in approaching problems.

"We know that other sea slugs like the sea hares release ink and toxins. But I've been seeking a way to find whether the nudibranchs would do the same when threatened. I wanted you here to watch what I've devised."

"Nudibranchs merely change color or swim away," she said. "Or taste so bad nothing would want to eat them."

"They may be more clever than that," Sidney said, adjusting some wires which led to electrodes in the tank. "I think they release invisible toxins that inhibit any predator from even considering them again. We can begin to find out now."

He lowered a rack of specially shaped small tubes into the tank over the colorful *Flabellina iodinea*, which now rested comfortably on the imitation sea floor.

"These tubes are designed to imbibe the water directly over the pretty little thing when it's threatened."

"Are you going to place a starfish next to it?"

"No," he smiled. "As you noted, *Flabellina* would only swim away. I'll give it a stimulus it can't escape."

He pointed to the wires into the tank.

"Electricity?" Cynthia looked appalled. "That will kill it."

"No, no," he said and chuckled. "It won't be happy but it won't die. I've found the right amount of current to get what I want. And this specimen is large enough to give us a significant sample of toxin—if there is any to be released."

"And in the process of finding the right current," she snapped, "how many died?" Sidney's cold stare silenced her.

"Some suffering is necessary for research to move ahead. Now watch." He fingered the rheostat and a light hum sounded. He abruptly turned the dial.

Cynthia gasped as the *Flabellina* writhed in agony. There was no escape from the current which filled the water with pain. Sidney quickly cut the current and the *Flabellina* slowly settled to the bottom of the tank, quite still, its colors no longer brilliant.

"It's only stunned. And those tubes above it captured the water at the same moment the shock came."

He removed the rack and handed it to Cynthia, who said nothing.

"Now be a good doctoral candidate and do your usual stellar analyses of the water in these tubes. You're very good at that. Write up your report and get it to me by the end of the week. We'll check the results with other samples of water I've taken—from similar experiments."

Cynthia nodded blankly, excused herself and left the room.

Little coward, Sidney thought. Whatever she found, if valuable, would make its way into his own research. If she found nothing she could use it in her own work, whatever it was she was studying. He paid little attention to the interests of other people, except noting their expertise in certain fields of research. He enjoyed sharing his genius with others, as with Cynthia, and use their talents as it suited him.

Sidney approached the locked room, his private experimental room, in a remote part of the research facility. His place of wonders, that one day would be known by the scientific world. But not yet. Much more needed to be done before that triumph could be enjoyed.

Powerful lights, approximating the sun, illuminated the room with the power of full daylight. At night the place would be plunged into darkness. The sun-bulbs were suspended over a gigantic glass-walled tank, fifteen feet on a side and six feet high, which filled the center of the large room. It was another simulated sea bottom, but much larger than that of the modest laboratory where other experiments were conducted.

Sidney walked to the tank. The water was translucent, allowing vision only at that portion of the tank where an observer stood. Stimulated by well-positioned circulators, the sea water rippled periodically. He looked closely, and with pride saw a colorful *Tochuina tetraquetra*, the orange-peel nudibranch, a full two feet long—over twice its normal length—gracefully coast along the bottom near him. Foraging. Constantly eating.

The well-stocked tank ensured that this gigantic sea slug, larger by far than anything that dwelt in the natural ocean, would not go hungry. Nor would any of the other giant occupants which shared this most special environment. It was a delicate task, making sure they were well fed. If not, they would devour each other. For unlike the sea hares, the large and well-known sea slugs, the nudibranchs were carnivorous. And if the need arose, cannibalistic.

Sidney approached the steps leading to a large platform at the level of the great tank's surface. A   tall refrigerator rested on the platform, as well as several tables for stages of his work. He removed a large container from the refrigerator and opened it. Inside lay some of the secrets of his success.

"A good diet for a good body and mind." His lifelong motto, which he successfully incorporated into his experiments. Nudibranchs fed on a variety of animals. Sponges, hydroids, corals, anemones, bryozoans and even barnacles fell to the sharp teeth and strong jaws of the shell-less, jellylike gastropods. However, Sidney Surient had guided his pets to enjoy a wider variety of dishes. In particular, mammalian flesh.

It was a wondrous discovery, and with careful preparation, a combined concoction of ground beef, lamb, and chicken found a welcome reception by Sidney's giant sea slugs. He thought of himself as expanding their horizons of dining, helping them enjoy the delight of new tastes. With growth hormone added, he had watched the creatures grow, and in the past two years, their enormous sizes were reached.

The water beneath him in the tank stirred and he spied his *Dendronotis iris* moving along the sea floor. Normally six inches in length, this giant dendronotid measure thirty-six, with a width of over a foot. Dark red in color, it somewhat resembling a monstrous caterpillar with numerous arm-like projections and tentacles. Sidney had captured great quantities of its toxins, and put them to good use in his research.

He spent over fifteen minutes preparing portions of the special supplemental meal for his creatures. Several large pieces of meat were always added to the ground mixture, to present a culinary challenge for the great sea slugs. Sometimes these tasty meals would satisfy the diners for days.

When he finished he took the supply of meat

dishes and walked around the tank, tossing his offerings into the tank. He enjoyed the voracious appetites of his pets. Once one honed in on a meat dish, the attack was assured, and the rippling sea slug advanced and settled on the piece with vigor.

After an hour of observation, creating records and filing data in the computerized research station, he was finished. He had fed his wonders. Now he was to feed himself. An intriguing call from the proprietor of Asian Extreme promised a culinary treat he could not miss. Perhaps the promised delight of several weeks past.

"Dr. Surient," said Nontawat Srisai. He smiled exuberantly at one of his most regular customers. "Delighted to see you. It has been over two weeks since your last visit."

The slightly built, impeccably dressed owner of the restaurant of exotic cuisine shook Sidney's hand warmly, and escorted him to Sidney's private table, by a window which commanded a panoramic view of the Pacific. It was always ready whenever he chose to dine at the Extreme.

"I have been quite busy, Nontawat," Sidney replied. "Several of my experiments, plus some lengthy work on my latest book demanded my presence long past any decent hour for dinner. *Forced* to dine at home most nights. How tedious. However, your phone call this morning so intrigued me that I closed the lab early in order to prepare myself for tonight's repast."

"I am so glad you could make it," Nontawat replied, as Sidney eased himself into a beautiful batik-cushioned chair, which proclaimed the comforts of the establishment. "You won't be disappointed, I assure you."

"Come now," Sidney said, "tell me what you have prepared. A specially imported live lobster from Japan? Eating them while they still live provides an exciting adventure for the taste buds. Or perhaps monkey? I haven't eaten decent monkey since my last trip to India."

"None of that," Nontawat replied. "May I sit?"

It was an unusual request. Sidney normally permitted no one sit at his level except close friends or business contacts. Yet if he planned to press partner-ship with Nontawat in the Extreme, it would do no harm.

"Certainly, Nontawat, certainly." He motioned to the chair across from him. On cue, a most expensive bottle of wine arrived.

"On the house, my friend," Nontawat said with a satisfied smile. Considering the quality of the drink, Sidney felt a thrill of excitement as to what would eventually accompany it. Some form of ocean life, but what would it be?

"Dr. Surient," Nontawat began. "You have been a faithful patron and friend since Asian Extreme opened. I want to speak with you about a business matter."

"I *am* interested in investing in Asian Extreme. You have a chance to expand your style of restaurant in many places, and I could be of immense help."

"I appreciate that. But I will speak with you only *after* you enjoy the special meal tonight. It will be served in a few moments. I want your honest evaluation of the dish. It's at the center of what I want to propose."

Sidney was delighted. Not only with anticipation at a new taste treat, but the chance to invest money, and make much more, in a field he was sure he could help develop. He knew many people in many places who would patronize a restaurant with a double menu. To serve standard dishes to the common folk, and exotic dishes of endangered species to another, more sophisticated class of patron.

Nontawat excused himself and soon a set of dishes arrived which exuded aromas that nearly made Sidney faint with pleasure. He had never scented such food. The main dish itself looked in many ways like the *Tochuina tetraquetra* he enjoyed when he brought Stuart Pekkah to the restaurant. But the flavor of this meat was much better, incredibly delicate, the consistency something like lobster and yet willing to melt in his mouth.

He studied some of the pieces in the warming plate, lightly sizzling in the sauce. This was assuredly a sea slug but not from something as small as *Tochuina*, which rarely reached more than ten inches. These fillets were from a much larger creature. But beyond his own unique experiments, size was not a characteristic of most sea slugs.

The taste enthralled him. How had Nontawat stumbled upon such a find? How was this marvelous taste achieved? It was the best meal of his life, and Sidney had eaten many, many meals.

"So, my friend, how was it?" Nontawat asked, appearing after Sidney devoured the last morsel on the plate.

"You have outdone yourself," Sidney replied, dabbing his lips with the napkin. "Exquisite is hardly an adequate word."

"I thought you'd be delighted," Nontawat replied, "and because of it, because you have tasted it, I have a proposition to make."

"I half-expected it," Sidney said. "Business, I would guess. Big business."

"Correct. Would you join me in my office for an after-dinner drink?"

Sidney accepted the request with well-hidden glee. So many questions filled his mind about the meal, about the source of the meal. Now, answers were at hand.

They relaxed in leather-bound chairs in Nontawat's office, which resembled a sophisticated lounge more than an office. Bamboo plants graced the walls, the lighting was soft, the paintings on the walls of contemporary Eastern origin, done with delightful color and style.

Once they had their drinks, Nontawat made his proposal.

"The meal—what do you think it was?"

"I wondered at first. The taste was undoubtedly *Tochuina*. But the size of the fillets—and the heavenly texture of the meat. What in the world was that?"

"I have encountered an incredibly diverse source of products for the Asian Extreme. From my own homeland, Thailand. It came to my attention several weeks ago, but naturally I needed to examine, test the products. I ordered portions of several exotic creatures. But of all the wonders this new supplier provides, the great *Tochuina* you sampled tonight is the best."

"So it *was Tochuina*! And you want me to help secure more from this supplier?"

"Yes. I wish to set up a permanent contract. But he is expensive. And thus I thought you might be—"

"Interested? Of course!" Sidney shifted his bulk to stare directly at Nontawat. "But on one condition. You *must* tell me where he is, and especially how he managed to gain access to such a monstrous sea slug. I must find out what his secret is, if he has managed to raise those beauties himself."

Nontawat was silent, his expression stoic.

"What's the difficulty?" Sidney asked. "My request is reasonable."

"No. It is not reasonable. I will not endanger my supplier by allowing too much knowledge to leak out. I will not divulge where he is specifically, and I have no idea how he manages to obtain such a creature as the *Tochuina* you tasted tonight. He insists on complete secrecy."

"Ridiculous. Tell me, or you can forget any investment on my part." Sidney was annoyed at such behavior.

"Then I was mistaken," Nontawat said flatly. "It is a good offer I am making, and would profit you immensely."

"Just tell me where he is and I will find out what I want to know myself. You don't have to be involved."

"But I *will* be, Dr. Surient. My supplier conducts business in a world which can come to pieces in a moment. If the wrong people were to discover him, the government of Thailand would jail him at once. It would jeopardize not only him but myself if I were to tell you his location."

"You're being foolish and unreasonable. I *must* find his secret. I *must*!"

Nontawat shook his head.

"Perhaps stricter measures will help loosen your tongue. Do you know that with one phone call I can contact certain authorities and close you down overnight?"

"You wouldn't. You patronize the Extreme on a regular basis."

"And there is no record of my visits. No paper trail. If pressed I can say I was pursuing the location of exotic restaurants on a crusade to end exploitation of earth's rare creatures. Tell me what I want to know."

Nontawat was stunned.

Sidney knew his threats struck home. "My offer stands. Refuse it and you can see your future. Blank."

Nontawat silently looked at the beautiful paintings on the office wall for many long moments. Sidney patiently waited, until Nontawat broke the silence.

"His name is Phaitoon Chutimant. I know very little of him, and I fear what he might do to me for revealing this information. He owns a resort hotel in Surat Thani, a small town in southern Thailand, which covers his more lucrative activity. I will inform him what I have done, in telling you."

"While you are at it, also inform him that I will be in Surat Thani next Thursday and that I expect him to greet me, provide a superb room for me, meet with me and provide the data I want. You know the consequences if you don't comply. Now that I know his name, he will suffer the same fate as you if he crosses me."

Nontawat mechanically nodded.

"Now as to that investment you mentioned, once I return from Surat Thani, we will talk further. I can put over fifty thousand dollars cash in you hand immediately, if things go right."

Sidney expected that news to brighten Nontawat, but the man again only gave a slight nod of his head. He clearly was not prepared to find Sidney so forceful—ruthless, some might call it. Sidney silently chuckled to himself with amusement. He did enjoy seeing people squirm when placed in uncontrollable circumstances. Something like the *Flabellina* in the electrode tank.

His measures were justified, for he had suddenly discovered something which mandated pursuit to its end. With what he discovered in Surat Thani, how Phaitoon Chutimant developed his giant sea slugs, he would advance his own research to new levels of acclaim. At the same time he entered the world of the restaurateur.

Sidney Surient luxuriated in the comfort of the great king-size bed in his room at the Resorte Extraordinaire, a plush hotel located on Ko Samui, one of the principal island destinations of southern

Thailand. Sidney was grateful that Nontawat was not quite correct when he said his supplier's resort hotel was in the town of Surat Thani. That place, located on the coast, was in Sidney's estimation tawdry and undesirable, being the hub of the exporting coconut and rubber. It was only a stopping off spot for trips to the *truly* beautiful sites further south or west, mountains and lush rainforest.

The real appeal of Surat Thani lay in its description as "the province of a thousand islands." A great number of islands did grace that part of the Gulf of Thailand, and many, such as Ko Samui, were playgrounds for the wealthy.

Sidney sipped his drink and relaxed in the soft breezes of the overhead fan. He was freshly showered and delighted in the smooth progression of his plans.

Ko Samui boasted an international airport, and Phaitoon Chutimant himself met Sidney when he deplaned on the lush island late that morning.

Sidney was prepared for some resistance to his forced arrival, considering the reluctance Nontawat displayed to disclose the name of the man who raised the largest sea slugs on the planet. Nothing could have been farther from the truth. Unlike the diminutive Nontawat and his frequently obsequious behavior, Phaitoon was a self-assured, distinguished figure, nearly as tall as Sidney, dressed with taste that Sidney admired. It was logical that Phaitoon would appear so, since his resort hotel catered only to those who could afford rooms that cost over twenty thousand Baht a night. It cost Sidney nothing of course, part of the clever plan he insisted upon.

Phaitoon was talkative and pleasant, well versed in matters both economic and scientific. Sidney more than once wondered why Nontawat was so hesitant about him. Phaitoon would make a far better business partner than Nontawat, and Sidney was already formulating ideas to completely cut out Nontawat and deal directly with Phaitoon.

It was evident that the Thai hotelier was extremely successful with his resort. Sidney guessed that his secret sideline, providing exotic creatures for the dinner delights of people both at home and abroad, must be a hobby.

At dinner earlier that evening, Sidney pressed the reason for his visit.

"As Nontawat no doubt informed you, it is the size of the *Tochuina* which arrested my attention, not only their exquisite taste. How do you do it? Gaining not only the remarkable size, but the unbeatable consistency and flavor?"

"Patience," Phaitoon replied. "I am still reluctant to tell you trade secrets. Guided with information from Nontawat, I have done a bit of research and found how you have an excellent reputation in the study of the nudibranchs. Whatever you publish gets much attention—you have even popularized the creatures to an amazing degree with the average citizen."

"Do not be concerned," Sidney assured him. "I know exactly how to present data in a compelling and safe way. Neither you nor your operation will come under any public scrutiny. I merely seek your methods of raising the slugs."

"I cannot and will not take unnecessary risks."

"Finances do not concern you," Sidney said, looking at the many guests in the large dining room. "But I can get you more money than Nontawat ever could. And can help you, if you choose, to expand your outlets in the United States."

This seemed to please Phaitoon, who quietly smiled. "I will conduct you to the farm," Phaitoon said. "But I warn you that I have not yet decided whether to disclose their special diet, by which my slugs get their size and flavor. "

This delighted Sidney to no end. He would see the slug farm. And then pressure Phaitoon, as he did to Nontawat. Sidney well knew that however wealthy the denizens of the third world might be, fear and money were potent weapons to bring them to their knees.

Their dinner ended on a pleasant note, and Phaitoon even promised to have a midnight snack sent to Sidney's room, as he requested. Phaitoon, he thought, might share Sidney's taste for all of the good things in life.

It was nearly midnight when he heard the knock at his door.

"Come in," he said in a loud voice, and the server entered, bearer of the midnight snack he desired. "And close the door behind you." The server complied.

Sidney looked at the server with pleasure. She could not be more than thirteen, and radiated both innocence and desire. Her face was beautiful, made up in the arousing, exotic way young Thai women could prepare themselves. She wore a diaphanous dress, and he could discern she wore nothing beneath it.

He motioned for her to come to him, and she readily complied. She was even more fetching as she stood by his bed, smiling. The server and the midnight snack were one. Sidney was going to have a most enjoyable feast.

The sun shone brightly the next day, and Sidney sipped coffee as he gazed out over the ocean from the balcony of his room at the Resorte Extraordinaire. Phaitoon himself would take Sidney by boat to one of the many islands he owned, where he raised the exotic animals which he provided for the menus of specialized restaurants.

With very little pressure at their dinner the previous night, Sidney learned from Phaitoon that it was not only sea slugs which occupied his list of offerings. Leopards, gibbons, and young tigers were raised on his farms, as well as species of endangered wild birds: the hawk-eagle, white-throated kingfishers and eclectus parrots. It was a treasure trove of creatures illegal to kill, and Phaitoon had them all. Sidney relished the idea of sampling meat from all of them eventually. His mouth watered at the prospect.

Phaitoon insisted that they wear simple clothing, so as to draw little attention. He assured Sidney that in spite of being a successful businessman, the Thai government would swoop down upon him in an instant if they had any idea of his "avocation".

After a delicious lunch, the two men approached a modest boat moored at the resort pier. Sidney was attired in beach jacket, shorts and sandals, as ordinary as he could get. A steady sea breeze promised a refreshing ride. Within moments the boat sped across the waves, and soon the resort was a fine white line on the horizon.

After half an hour they neared a palm-covered island with a small mountain in its center. "We are here," Phaitoon announced. "My island of farms."

They moored the boat at a small pier. No one was in sight.

"I dismissed the staff for the early afternoon," Phaitoon said. "It is best that as few people as possible know of my—business partners."

"Wise, wise decision," Sidney said. However, he was not naïve to the ways of the world, especially the illegal world. Phaitoon might be a model of business efficiency and polite behavior. However, if he tried any unwise action against Sidney, a small gun rested in the pocket of Sidney's jacket, and he was an excellent shot. Should Phaitoon give him trouble he would kill him and raid the secrets of his slug farm.

They walked a short distance on a path through tropical foliage, and soon approached a large wooden building near the water. It was weathered with age, but stood strong and sturdy.

"My slug farm," he announced. "Within the walls of this unpretentious building."

They entered, and Phaitoon flicked on the lights. They were not bright but gave sufficient illumination.

"My electric system on the island is important and I choose not to drain it unnecessarily," Phaitoon explained.

"True," said Sidney. "Now where is the farm?"

He led the way to a vast opening in the floor of the building, at least twenty feet square. "It is there," Phaitoon explained, indicating the waters in the open space.

Sidney peered into the depths of the tank, which appeared to extend under the floor on all sides. "I don't see anything," Sidney said flatly. "I'm not in the mood for humor or tricks."

"You are so incredibly impatient, Dr. Surient. Watch."

Phaitoon walked to a small stand on a dais at one end of the tank. He flicked several switches mounted on the stand. At once blue lights flickered beneath the water, giving a fully illuminated view of the simulated sea bottom. At once Sidney saw them.

Five monstrous *Tochuina* stirred to life from their resting places on the floor of the tank. They glided with grace over the floor of the ocean environment. Sidney gasped at their size, for each was at least five feet in length.

"Amazing! They are simply amazing," he said, almost breathless with awe. "You have accomplished a biological wonder here."

As the sea slugs undulated in a circular motion around the tank, Sidney rose to his full stature. "All right, Phaitoon. How have you done this? Out with it!"

"As I carefully explained, I am not ready to—"

"Quit stalling!" Sidney ordered. "It is clear to me that you wish to do business with me, and I am certainly willing to do business with you. If you need to see my money to prove I am serious—"

"That is not it, Dr. Surient. I have reservations, for you might unwittingly advertise what I have accomplished, and what I do with what I have accomplished."

"Bullshit," Sidney said. "I will not invest until I know how you have done it. I did not fly to this miserable little country of yours in order to be put off."

"And if I refuse? After all, you have seen the creatures. You know they will be available for whatever restaurants I choose to sell them."

"I demand you tell me your secret," Sidney ordered. "I have many contacts, and will not hesitate to use them. As with your little friend Nontawat, it would not be to your advantage to have your industry revealed to the authorities."

"I expected as much from you," Phaitoon said calmly. " All right, I will tell you. I feed them . . . meat. Fresh meat. Dogs, cats, fish, whatever I choose to give them. They have developed a great appetite, and with that appetite has come their size."

"Do not toy with me," Sidney warned. "I have done exactly the same with my experiments, but I have not achieved this size."

Phaitoon sighed. He went to a large container on the opposite side of the tank. Out of it he retrieved several large pieces of meat, and tossed them into the waters of the great container. Sidney was astonished as the great slugs attacked the meat and soon devoured it. Unlike his specimens, the meat did not have to be minced. The small colony circled more slowly after they ate, searching for more.

"Amazing reflexes," Sidney said. He stared into the depths of the tank as the slugs settled to the bottom, apparently satiated. Then he noticed a shape in the rocks and undersea foliage. He studied the form. It looked familiar.

"What is that?" he asked. "Next to those rocks—my God! It's a femur. A human femur!"

Phaitoon nodded grimly as he walked to Sidney and stood beside him, staring into the tank. "Yes, I am afraid so. It is all that remains of one of my workers, who once cared for the *Tochuina*."

"What happened?"

"Sanjay was always drunk, or close to it. Apparently one day he was here alone, feeding the residents of the farm, and he stumbled into the tank. We found what was left of him in the tank the next day. The slugs had feasted."

"They ate him?"

"And that, Dr. Surient, is when I discovered that the *Tochuina* have a great taste for human flesh. I have managed to make that a regular part of their diet. After that sad incident with Sanjay, the slugs began to grow even larger—and I found that their flesh became incredibly tasty. Hence my success."

Sidney was at first appalled. But an idea immediately formed as to how he could apply the same principle to his work. So many homeless people, so many wandering children, so many people who walked with no protection. A supply of cuisine for his own nudibranchs. A source of further research which he would divulge when he could mask his success with other data.

"Thank you for your information," Sidney stated.

"It is unfortunate you will never use it," Phaitoon replied.

"What do you mean?" Sidney snapped. He was ready to get his gun.

"Your tendency to become publicly noticed is a danger to us," Phaitoon went on. "Your culinary interests attract too much attention. Your research would eventually lead to the discovery of our operation—"

"Don't be absurd," Sidney said. "And don't threaten me. I have already warned you—"

"A warning duly noted," Phaitoon calmly replied. "And a final reason for what must take place."

With a deft move Phaitoon pushed Sidney with all his might and with a squeal Sidney slipped over the edge into the waters of the tank.

"You bastard!" he shouted, splashing in the water. "You'll regret—"

He screamed as pain seared up his right leg. In the water he could faintly see that one of the *Tochuina* had fastened itself to his right leg. Then another attacked his other leg.

Desperately he struggled, realizing what was happening. He struggled against the slugs but soon sank beneath the waters, his pain blurring as liquid filled his lungs. The water soon colored red, but not from any toxins released by the sea slugs. Sidney provided the coloration himself.

Phaitoon shook his head somewhat sadly as he walked to the door of the building and clicked off the overhead lights. The lights of the tank remained burning. For some reason they stimulated the appetites of his amazing farm animals.

Business was sometimes messy. Necessary precautions always ready to be employed. He returned to his craft at the small dock. The boating accident would be reported at once, as to how Dr. Sidney Surient became violently ill and fell overboard, sinking before he could be saved.

Strange, he also reflected. Sidney Surient would now visit many restaurants of the world, as part of the *Tochuina* which would eventually be harvested and sold. And persons of excellent taste would marvel at the wondrous dishes, prepared to satisfy their very unique appetites.

The Naked Garden
or
Artemis Versus the Slugs
Mary Stuart Jacobi

This story is set in the same universe as the forthcoming *I, Bonita* series. In order to fully appreciate it, a little background information is required. The *I, Bonita* series includes: *Big Witch on Campus, The Saint of Ste-Foy* and *Goddess on the Infield.* The first two books detail the account of an immortal witch's experience on a modern liberal arts campus. It is difficult for any new teacher to adapt to the madcap politics of a Jesuit university in the city of Quebec. But when that lecturer happens to be a centuries-old pagan priestess who looks younger than her own students, a lot of cultural confusion is likely to ensue. This story "The Naked Garden or Artemis versus the Slugs" is but a slice from the layer cake that is the third novel: *Goddess on the Infield.* There is no such thing as an ordinary day in the life of an immortal. One in which she is assisting her new acolyte in the ways of the Goddess is certainly unusual. Remember: Whom the gods employ, they first make mad.

Mary Stuart Jacobi
Kildare, Eire 2006

Cela est bien dit réspondit Candide
mais il faut cultiver notre jardin.
—Voltaire (1694-1778), *Candide*

Oleeysheef!" My dog-girl uttered in a muffled growl.

"Oily sheep?" I echoed. "Take that newspaper out of your mouth, young lady! I cannot comprehend a word you are saying."

"Holy Shit!" Artemis articulated in English.

"I seriously doubt that such words form this morning's headline," I told my disciple.

"No really, Bonnîe!" she implored. "Like I mean shit!"

"Do you actually touch your chalice with those lips?"

"Kiss my athame." Artemis snarled under her breath.

"The sense of hearing among Our Kind is many times better than mortals," I cautioned her. "You had better appreciate that fact now that you have become one of Us."

Fortunately it was still in the good hour of a Saturday morning. Few of my neighbors were as early to rise as Father Pompeux who lived in the campus rectory next door. His dog took the old Jesuit scholar for his morning constitutional all the earlier during the long summer days in the City of Québec. I sensed that no one was watching so I summoned the morning paper through the air into my hand. The newsprint was damp with dew and human saliva. I dried it with mental microwaves. "The paperboy keeps missing my porch," I observed.

"I swear your grass wasn't this green yesterday!" she murmured

"One would think that in a Province where every *jeune homme* aspires to be the next star forward of *les Nordiques*, the little snot could put it through the goal!" I continued.

"I would have brought it to you," she complained.

"Of what is the use in having a lycanthropic acolyte if she would rather sniff dog droppings than fetch the morning paper?" I bemoaned.

"I heard that!" she proved my earlier point for me.

She was having difficulty adapting to her new condition, but there was nothing wrong with her heightened sense of hearing.

"Some dog crapped on your flagstones Bonnîe."

My protégé thrust a pale forefinger in the direction of the offending deposit.

"That was no dog," I qualified. "That was Bonaparte."

"*Napoleon* shit on your walkway?" she wondered aloud.

"*Canis stulta*," I tisked. "Bonaparte is Father Pompeux's dog. Actually, the creature is not so much a dog as a dust mop with delusions of grandeur."

"How do you know it was him?" she asked as she loitered over the befouled flagstone.

"I do not have to smell that bloody thing," I stated. "It is a simple question of scale. Russian wolfhounds deliver manifestos, German shepherds dictate statements, Lhasa apsos drop commas. Artemis McAffe, pull your dress back down this instant!"

The teenager looked up at me with those salt sea eyes in surprise. As she jerked her head up, her long copper curls wigwagged about her shoulders. Her hair had doubled in length during the past forty-eight hours. At a loss as to what to do with such luxuriant growth, she had tied it into a pair of long poodle ears with bright pink Scuncis to keep them out of her way.

"Guinevere, heel!" I addressed the girl by the name of her recently deceased playmate.

Artemis assumed a starting gate position on all fours. Such was the motor memory of a ghost greyhound. I had yet to come to an accommodation with the odd habits of a young woman whose right cerebral hemisphere was possessed by the spirit of a dead dog. She was still shaken from her own near-death experience in the recent automobile accident that had claimed her beloved pet's life.

My Goddess had long ago telepathically presented me with Her Bronze Age memories of having performed the sacred Minoan bull dance on the island of Thera. She had become one with the Minotaur, and so vicariously had I. Utilizing the same method I had once gifted an Iowa medicine woman with the life impressions of the mystic white buffalo. Indeed I have given and received many memory downloads over the centuries, but I had never before bequeathed a dog's life on a human being.

"On your feet or on your knees, but not down on all fours!" I commanded. "Many women become bitches, but few bitches become women."

The girl hesitated. If I hadn't intervened she might have left her own calling card on top of Bonaparte's so as to assert her territorial claim to my front yard. I slapped the rolled up newspaper into my open palm to get her attention. As I did so a brown object the size and shape of a cigar arced several metres and slapped wetly upon the flagstone in front of Artemis.

"More Bonaparte?" Asked my half-hound

houseguest as she crawled forward to inspect this new delivery.

"*Non*," I stated. "It appears to be a *Prophysaon andersoni.*"

"What's a prophylactic and son?" Artemis mangled the Latin name.

"It is a species of slug that is common to eastern Canada," I replied. "It appears that I inadvertently poached the poor bugger when I dried out the paper."

"Yuck!" Artemis wrinkled her pixie nose. "Like I had that newspaper in my *mouth*?" She gagged in revulsion. "I think I'm gonna hurl!"

"A parboiled slug disgusts you, yet you find dog stools fascinating?" I inquired.

"I hate slugs!" she declared.

"*Porquoi*?" I asked.

"I once tried to eat one," she reflected. "When I started foaming at the mouth, my mistress went for her shotgun. She was about to put me down until I rolfed it up into my doggie dish."

"That was not you, Artemis," I corrected her. "That is one of Guinevere's memories."

"Oh," she mulled, "sometimes I forget."

"Stand up child!" I demanded. "You are getting grass stains on my white gown."

Artemis looked between her arms and remembered that she was wearing one of my imported Pakistani dresses minus the puffy pantaloons. She rose unsteadily upon her hindquarters. There was part of her brain that was unused to being a biped.

"What about the poop?" she inquired.

"The Expos are doing so poorly this season I might as well wrap it in the sports section," I proposed. "Then again I have a better idea."

I levitated the offending deposit to the proper height of my strike zone.

"The batter is up to the plate!" I announced. "Here is the wind up, and it is good!"

I delivered a haymaker to the unsavory little door prize.

"It is a hard drive over center field and it is out of the park!" I continued.

I sent it sailing onto the front step of the rectory.

"And the crowd goes wild!" Artemis proclaimed.

She clapped her hands together as she bounced up and down in a little happy dance I had witnessed the late Guinevere perform.

"*Turpis fugit!*" I mused.

"That's more fun than catching Frisbees in my teeth!" she announced.

"Back in the house!" I ordered. "I have a hard enough time explaining my own eccentric behavior to the off-campus mundanes without one of my students hiking up her skirts and using my lawn as a lavatory!"

"Sore-ee." Artemis apologized in her broad Nova Scotia accent.

She meekly hung her head and attempted to hide her face behind her hair. Her accelerated hair growth was a by-product of the process of immortalization. I had inadvertently bestowed eternal life to the girl when I had faith healed the injuries she had sustained in the car accident that had claimed the life of her dog. Because I did not know my own strength, it was now my responsibility to introduce this gosling to an existence she could have never imagined.

I ushered Artemis inside my cottage. I had to apply my newspaper to her bubble backside as incentive when she began to snort at the wisteria arbor for the spore of my cat. My striped tabby had made himself scarce since I had introduced a fifty kilogram bipedal puppy into our happy little home. He instinctively knew that the gal was not what she seemed.

"Why do you let the University Chaplain relieve his dog on your property?" Asked Artemis.

I willed the door to close behind us.

"I am certain that he does it just to vex me. This rented cottage is technically the property of the University. Father Pompeux seems to think it is therefore open range.

I would prefer that he seize and decease," I lamented, "but I would be satisfied if he just honored the court order that keeps him twenty metres away from me."

"How long has there been a court order?"

"Since he denounced me as a witch at commencement last month," I answered.

"Why does he hate you so much?" she wondered. "Like he threw holy water in your face!"

"He fears me because I am a *ban-druí*," I replied. "An anointed pagan priestess threatens his tribal phallocracy."

"What about Bonaparte?" she insisted.

"Try to get a dog to obey an injunction," I mused. "I suppose that if he did not have Bonaparte as his privy proxy, he would be dropping trou on my doorstep as you just attempted to. Pompeux officially denies that it's the work of that ludicrous fur ball of his."

"Hey!" Artemis protested. "I used to be a fur ball!"

"*Non ma jeune fille*," I corrected. "Thou art a pink primate! Guinevere was the one with the fawn coat."

"Okay!" she pleaded.

"While I am making this distinction, there will be no marking of your territory around here!" I demanded.

"I get it Bwana!" she implored. "*Vous ta zone moi chienne!*"

"And snuffling about my bushes is *right out!*"

"Okay! Okay! No snuffling your bush."

This girl could be a trial at times.

"Off with the gown!" I announced with a snap of my fingers. "I could clean it by ultrasound with you in it, but I fear what effect the vibrations might have on your inventive bladder."

"You don't have to rub it in," she retorted as she pulled the garment up over her head.

I quickly drew the Venetian blinds that hung across the room from where I stood. The front window would have presented an unobstructed view of my nubile companion to anyone passing on the street. Artemis' metamorphosis had removed the midge storms of freckles from her all over her Celtic body leaving her skin as white as a crocus in the snow. She was now so porcelain pale that her red hair and blue eyes looked as though they had been painted onto a bisque doll. Although ghostly pallid, she had become beautiful beyond all mortal definition of beauty.

"So how do you do this sonic cleaning?" she asked as she handed over the dress.

"Look, Rock," I gestured, "nuthin' up my sleeve." With a flick of my wrists, I snapped the garment out like a white linen sheet. All the grass stains and grime from the yard instantly vanished.

"Neat trick," she demurred as she held out her hand.

"You shall not need this today," I replied as I laid it over the back of a comfy chair.

"Fine by me," she readily agreed, "you know I'm a born again naturist."

"I shall not require these either," I stated as I

began to remove my own white habit.

"So what're we going to do," she asked, "commune with the Goddess?"

"Indeed we shall Daughter of Diana," I affirmed.

"Shall I set the altar and light the candles?" she inquired.

"*Non*," I responded. "We are going to perform a devotion to the Goddess of a more earthly nature."

She looked me up and down. She had only seen my body previously during her coven's fire leaping sacrament on the eve of the summer solstice. On that occasion we had all looked red and out of focus.

"Okay," she said with a wry smile on her soft pink lips. "You're the best friend I've ever had and I still haven't thanked you for saving my life."

She coyly shrugged in her slender shoulders.

"I haven't gone with a chick since I was shooting porn to stay off the streets. I've never done with a girl as pretty as you are, Bonnîe. It sure doesn't hurt that you're built like a brick shithouse!"

She blushed and winked.

I smiled when I realized the nature of her misunderstanding.

"I thank you for the compliment . . . I think, but it is not *that* kind of devotion," I assured her.

I pulled the pin from my brown hair and let it cascade down to the small of my back.

"So then like why are we standing naked together

in your living room?" she asked with a puzzled inflection.

"Because we shall proceed immediately to my garden," I answered.

I summoned her toward the backdoor.

"Do you always do your gardening naked?" she asked as we reemerged into the summer morning.

"Always," I assured her.

"Even when you were living in that convent in Europe?" she queried.

"All of my Immortal Sisters communed with the sun in this manner behind Our cloistered walls," I related.

"Cool!" she exclaimed as she opened her limbs wide to receive the welcoming rays of the Atten. She became a female version of the famous Leonardo drawing. She was woman, the measure of all things.

We stood side by side, clasped hands and took in deep cleansing breaths.

"I love to feel the warm kiss of Lugh upon my skin," I expressed.

"Too bad I lost my supply of organic sun block in the accident." my protégé lamented.

"Put all that behind you," I informed her, "you shall never tan, burn or peel ever again."

"How come?" she asked.

"Your immortal body now has almost immeasurable recuperative powers," I answered. "No matter how fair you are your skin cells will repair themselves faster than ultraviolet light can damage them."

"Cool," she repeated.

We stood in silence for several moments as the full disc of the sun cleared the top of my high stone garden walls. As we bathed in its beneficent brilliance, Artemis looked me over with a sidelong glance.

"So how come I didn't get tits like yours when I went through this transformation?" she asked. She cupped her maidenly breasts with her palms. "I've got two fried eggs and you have ripe pears.

"It doesn't work that way," I responded with a knowing smile.

"How come?" she wanted to know.

"The process of immortalization does not change you so much as enhance you," I explained. "It takes your existing genetic inheritance and emphasizes certain characteristics and mutes others."

"Like for instance?"

"The reason that your freckles vanished in one night is due to the fact that the polarity of the dominant gene you carry for skin pigmentation was reversed," I explained.

"How does that happen?"

"Much of the DNA in your cells codes for nothing in particular. This so-called 'junk DNA' often contains lines of code that instructs the protein factories in your nuclei to disregard previous lines of code."

"Like what?"

"Every woman in the world has as many hair follicles on her skin as a chimp or a gorilla. We all possess *codons* that tell our bodies to grow coats of fur."

"Like you're kidding right?"

"*Non ma chéri*. With a few rare exceptions we have more recently evolved genes that countermand these more ancient orders. They subsume them completely, or they tell our bodies to delay the growth of hair in certain places until sex hormones trigger their growth during puberty."

"But my thatch now looks like a twelve-year-old's!" she complained. "So does yours."

"Bluntly put," I surmised, "but essentially correct. The same is true for our armpits. All of Our Kind are like that. It's just the way it is."

"You mean my floss is going to stay this way?"

"Just how many vulgar euphemisms do you Anglophones have for pubic hair?"

"Bush, thatch, beaver, pelt, short hairs, muff, muffin, merkin," she rattled off. "How many do you want?"

"That will be more than sufficient."

"Why ask?"

"The human species has evolved through a process called neotony. This is the course of retaining infantile characteristics in the adult life form. We

Immortal Primes represent the vanguard of the next step in human evolution. You will just have to get used to the way you presently look at eighteen. If the Goddess wills, it shall be how you will appear when you are eight hundred."

Artemis crossed her arms across her small bosom and shivered despite the warm summer sun.

"I'm scared," she admitted. "So much has happened to me all so sudden."

I gave her delicate hand a reassuring squeeze.

"*Cher* Artemis, in time you will be able to consciously control all of your autonomic nervous functions," I enlightened her.

"What does that mean?"

"You shall not perspire, blush, develop gooseflesh or shiver unless you want to."

"Eventually you will be able to fool any polygraph machine devised by man."

"What else?"

I looked away for a moment and then responded. "Well, I have not experienced a menstrual period in the past one hundred and fifty years."

"Say what!"

"They are such a bother that I prefer not to have them."

"Does that mean we can't have babies?"

"Of course we can," I answered, "but only when we want to. I can trigger ovulation at will. I can also chose whether or not to allow a fertilized ovum to be implanted in my uterus. Immortality does have its perks you know."

Artemis leaned toward me and sniffed my neck.

"Is that why you smell like. . . ." She did not complete the sentence.

"Like what?" I prompted.

"Don't take this the wrong way Bonnîe," she proposed hesitantly, "but the doggie part of me thinks you're in heat."

"Oh, that," I realized what she was leading to. "My metabolic rest state is that of a woman who is perpetually ovulating. Most women are in that condition for only a few days each month. I am that way twenty-four/seven, moon after moon, century upon century. It drives men out of their skulls when we are at close quarters. That is why I tend to avoid the companionship of males."

"Christ!" she exclaimed. "Like I've heard of the Singing Nun and *The Flying Nun*, but I've never heard of the Ovulating Nun before!"

"We each have our bare to cross," I said with a shrug.

"Is that why you look so plush?" she asked.

"*Pardon?*"

"I mean, look at you. That set of pouty lips, two rosy cheeks and a pair of doughnut sized—"

I cut her off in mid-sentence. "*Oui*," I conceded.

"Those features are all symptomatic of my condition."

"Will I also loose my belly button?" she pointed toward my unblemished midriff.

"It is one of the final manifestations of the transformation," I assured her. "Be patient. You shall have all the time in the world to adjust to your new body, Goddess willing."

"But I'm as white as a calla lily!" she exclaimed.

"*Manibus date lilia plenis*," I quoted Virgil. "Let us now concentrate on buds of a different sort. You have shown me yours, now I shall show you mine."

I drew her forward by the hand.

"I've always loved your garden." Said Artemis. "Oh my goddess!"

She froze in mid step.

"*Le problème*?" I asked. "You act as though you had never seen flowers before."

"I've never seen flowers that vibrate like a neon jukebox!" she exclaimed. "Did you drop acid in my cocoa this morning?"

"It is all coming from inside your head. The active ingredient in the cocoa releases an opiate-like chemical in your brain called norepinepherone," I explained. "Your new immortal brain has more seratonin receptors than before."

"Are you telling me that I can get stoned on chocolate?"

"I paraphrase what Montezuma once told Our

Sister Nixia Albina in 1521: Chocolate is the catnip of the gods," I replied.

"Is that why all the flowers are all dancing around like fireflies?" she wondered.

"*Non*," I answered. "Describe what you are seeing."

"They're all glowing like someone turned on a black light at a rave," she stated. "They're like the stuff that makes jellyfish and foxfire glow in the dark."

"Bioluminescence?"

"Yeah!" she concurred. "They look like they're at the end of one of those tubes filled with cut glass that's all sparkly and such."

"A kaleidoscope?" I suggested.

"That's it!"

"You are seeing the world through new eyes," I informed her. "We immortals are tetrachromate."

"What does that mean?"

"Your eyes are now mixing ultraviolet light with the three wavelengths you have previously experienced," I said in response. "You now see flowers the way pollinating insects see them."

"Cool!"

"Just wait till tonight *ma chéri*," I promised. "The Milky Way glows like *le Champs Elysée*."

"How'd you get it all your flowers to start blooming so early this spring?"

"I tricked the plants into believing they were

rooted in South Carolina rather than southern Québec," I told her. "You can throw away the zonal charts for planting when you enter one of my gardens. Essentially I am hot-housing without a roof. I microwave the soil well below the root systems so that the ground is many degrees warmer than the surrounding landscape."

"Wow!"

"Then of course I can cheat," I confided.

"How?"

"Observe."

I directed three fingers toward the climbing clematis that had threaded its way up a latticework trellis attached to the eastern wall. This was the high barrier that blocked any view of my garden from the adjacent windows of the rectory. It had spared Father Pompeux from many a splendid sight as I had puttered over my plants *au naturel* during the spring.

"These flowers are heliotropic, that means they turn to face the sun during the day. I can accelerate their response time."

I clicked my fingers solely for dramatic effect. Each four petal violet cluster opened up and craned its neck toward the southern sky.

"That's wild!" Artemis opined. "I've only seen that happen in time lapse nature films."

"That was nothing," I replied. "Watch those lupines."

"You really have a lot of purple flowers Bonnîe."

"*Inceptis gravibus plerumque et magna professis Purpureus, late qui splendeat, unus et alter Adsuitar pannus.*"

"Works of serious promise and grand promises often have a purple patch or two stitched on to shine far and wide." Artemis surmised. "What the hell does that supposed to mean?"

"It is a quotation from the *Ars Poetica* by Horace," I informed her.

"But I don't know Latin!"

"*Au contraire ma chéri,*" I contradicted her. "We have been speaking it on and off all morning."

"Since when did I learn Latin?"

"I downloaded it into your brain last night. Along with Classical Greek and Hibernic Gaelic."

"Oh," she uttered as though I had just admitted to polishing her toenails while she slept.

"Are you sure you don't have too many purple flowers?"

"Allow me to explain Bonnîe's First Law of Chromatics," I replied.

"Okay." Her long ponytails bobbled like dog's ears as she cocked her head to listen.

"You can never have too much purple!" I proclaimed. "Allow me to demonstrate."

A stand of lupines began to tremble. Their palmate fronds shivered like cellophane as their pithy stalks prescribed a spiral motion in the air. The flowers in their grape-like spikes deepened from subdued blue into a saturated royal purple as they grew and opened.

"Righteous!" Artemis announced as she slapped her hand into my palm.

"I have just compressed several weeks' worth of accelerated growth into a few seconds," I explained.

"Ooh Yuck!"

"What is amiss?" I asked.

Artemis pointed a quivering finger at the newly matured flowers. Their stalks were writhing with mobs of slimy mollusks.

"I guess I do not know my own strength."

"What do you mean?"

"There must have been egg masses under the leaves," I surmised. "Hundreds of tiny eggs developed into fully grown slugs along with the lupines."

Artemis hugged her shoulders defensively.

"I am not going to let a zillion sloppy slugs lick me to death! Can't you get rid of them?"

"Pickling the little buggers in beer is the organic way to do it," I suggested.

"So pop open some brewskis!" she urgently appealed.

She hung her fingernails on her clenched teeth.

"Unfortunately my last houseguest was a young woman with an alcohol dependency problem," I recounted. "I had to pour my small supply of wine down the drain to ensure that she'd dry out."

"What a waste!" she stated.

"Not completely," I added. "I sacrificed my best cooking sherry to the oak tree in the front yard. Unfortunately Pompeux saw me do it!"

"Do something!" she pleaded. "They're stampeding! They'll eat everything in sight!"

Her toes curled reflexively as she looked down toward her nether regions.

"Unclench you buttocks *ma chéri*. The velocity of a slug is measured in centimeters per hour. I may have inadvertently accelerated their growth rate, but I didn't turn them into track stars. I estimate that the slimy tide will wash over your feet sometime around noon."

"I'm not waiting!" she hopped from one foot to another as though she were standing on a hotplate.

"Fire walk with me."

I stepped over to the nearest lupine. It was so weighed down by mustard coloured mollusks that it looked like a ripe banana plant. The stalk drooped and the fronds dripped with foamy yellow slime. I extended a forefinger and beckoned a slug to come aboard.

"Yeesh!" she said with a cringe. "If I did that I would never masturbate with that finger again!"

"I shall choose to ignore that remark."

I turned my attention back to my new friend.

"*Allô ma amie,*" I greeted it. "I will love you and squeeze you call you Georgette."

"How do you know that damned thing is female?" Artemis demanded.

"All slugs are hermaphrodites," I answered. "I once knew one intimately."

"A *slug*?" she said incredulously.

"*Non,* an hermaphrodite. I addressed her in the feminine even though all three sexes of her species lack external genitalia."

"Something tells me I'm not ready for this one."

"Something tells you rightly."

"Just keep that ooky thing away from me." Artemis recoiled from my approach.

I stroked the little creature's leathery mantle as it stretched to full length along my finger.

"Slugs are a part of the great web of life," I asserted. "They are as precious to Gaia as birds or butterflies."

"Birds don't slide around on their guts," she protested.

"Do snails bother you?" I asked.

"No."

"Slugs are essentially snails without shells," I explained. "Have you ever eaten escargot?"

"No, and I'm not going to!" she insisted. "I'm vegan now."

"So you are willing to dispatch them but not eat them?"

"Can't you just make them go poof or something?"

"Oh, very well," I acquiesced. "If thine slugs offend thee, cast them out!"

"Where are you going to send them?"

I looked down at Georgette and then toward the wall that adjoined the rectory property.

"I think I know of a good home for them," I suggested. "*Pardon moi ma Georgette*. Parting is slug sweat sorrow."

I turned toward the flowerbed and addressed the troops.

"*Attention!*"

A thousand little brown blobs perked up their antennae.

"No poor dumb sluggard ever won a war by dying in the country! She won it by making that bothersome pastor cry for this conjuring!"

The vast host began to levitate. They made little slurping puckering noises as their sticky feet disengaged from the foliage. The popping sounded like a sheet of bubble wrap.

"Those who are about to fly, I salute you!" I delivered a snappy salute.

Artemis clapped her hands together in delight. This was getting good.

"Fly my pretties! Fly!" I gave the command with a

wave of my arm.

The slugs retracted their eyestalks so that they looked as though they were all wearing little aviator goggles. They began to rise in quartets, forming flights as they ascended into a circular holding pattern over the centre of the garden. The flights gathered into groups and assembled into combat boxes such as those I had seen scissor the skies over Europe during the air war against the Third Reich. The space enclosed by my high garden walls was filled with a swirling vortex of slug flesh with the two of us standing at the epicentre.

"Tora! Tora! Tora!" I shouted.

Wave after wave of aerial mollusks arced high overhead and disappeared over the top. I linked elbows with Artemis and began singing "We'll Meet Again" in the manner of Vera Lynn. My companion did not now the words to this parting song from World War II, but she hummed along with me in her lovely new singing voice in between bursts of giggling.

"What's that?" she asked.

Her ears perked up at a racket that sounded like bird guano slapping against a windscreen.

"It sounds as though the Fighting 69th has finally reached the stone wall," I surmised.

"You sent them on a kamikaze mission?" My friend anxiously conjectured.

"Not exactly," I replied. "Do you want to see?"

"Like I'm supposed to pay a visit to the parish priest in my birthday suit?" she asked.

"You would be wasted on him," I explained.

"Permit me to levitate you up to the edge so you can peek over the wall," I offered.

"Sounds fun!" she replied as the wind I had summoned rippled through her shining hair.

She was already off the ground before she had finished her statement.

"Wee!" she squealed in delight as she began to rise above the garden. "It's like dancing on a cloud!"

"You are essentially correct," I corroborated. "I have condensed the volume of a blimp into a column of air the size of a mattress. I am bleeding off the heat of the tremendous head of barometric pressure I am confining beneath you, otherwise your feet would be glowing like coals."

"Whatever."

"Do not be so complacent," I cautioned her. "If I were to release my concentration, you would spurt upward as though you had been shot out of a cannon."

"Cool!"

"I do not think the neighborhood is prepared for a shocking pink skyrocket," I opined.

"Wee!" she exclaimed. "It's like a trampoline!"

Artemis executed a series of tucks and somersaults. She tried out a new acrobatic maneuver on each bounce. Her hair whirled about her like the tails of twin comets. She was so completely trusting that I would not drop her that she lost herself in joy. It was for such humble examples of courage and devotion as this that I felt reassured that fortune had favored the right young woman to share my eternal condition.

"How is the view?" I inquired from below her.

"Great!" she declared. "How about you?"

I almost lost my composure.

"If you make me laugh we are both liable to become airborne!" I cautioned her. "Then what will the neighbors say?"

"Father Pompeux isn't saying much of anything right now." *Bounce.* "He's just standing at the window with his mouth hanging open." *Bounce.* "Now he's crossing himself." *Bounce.* "Holy cow!" Artemis exclaimed on the rebound. "All of the slugs have spelled out something in big letters across the rectory windows!"

"That was the idea," I confirmed.

"Like what the hell does G-O-D-D-A-B mean?" (*I translate from the French*).

"It is supposed to be read from Pompeux's point of view," I replied. "You are reading it backwards."

"Oh." She mulled.

Then Artemis began to laugh hysterically.

Maïlong's Tale

Angie Ruth

I am trapped.

Neng, that unskilled magician, that . . . *excuse* for a magician had more cunning than I had anticipated. Now, I writhe, nearly helpless, in the bottom of a bowl, my powers dissipated.

There is a girl here. I have felt her presence before. She hides behind her hair, yet her thoughts are crystalline. She, too, is a prisoner here. And, like me, she hates Neng as much as I do.

He trapped me with a game, an *illusion*! I should have anticipated this. He has sought to capture me since our first encounter when he was yet a boy. Would that my vanity had not betrayed me today. I fear all is lost.

What am I? Smooth and a little . . . slimy. This is no state for a dragon to be in. His ugly face appears over the bowl's rim and he laughs. Confined in a cage of metal I cannot reach the water that will enable me to draw my power within myself once again. My only hope is that the other dragons will sense my danger and act on my behalf.

But I fear it is hopeless.

There is a girl here. Suseri she is called. A servant to the magician, she performs the duties of maid, cook and assistant—the latter consisting of tasks that are too difficult for her small hands.

Mostly, Suseri hides behind her hair, a blending of midnight and silk. There is no loyalty in her eyes. She fears the magician, but not as much as she hates him. Neng is a fool. Fear is a temporary binder. And hate cannot be contained.

Suseri gives me the most gentle care. Each day she lines my cage with her hair and feeds me grains of rice and bits of greens. When Neng is occupied, she sings to me and recounts tales of heroic dragons who have helped her people. I do not think she knows some of those tales are about me.

And how could she? Who would suspect the great Mailong foolish enough to fall for such a simple illusion? The most magnificent shape in the universe transmuted into a slug, waiting for Neng to destroy me and take my power. And what will become of my people then? What will become of Suseri?

Sometimes, Suseri weeps when she looks upon me; I feel a great loss. Once, I could have inspired tears of awe. Once, I could have repaid her kindness by presenting her with the most magnificent pearl ever created. But I have no power here.

The days pass. Suseri relates Neng's plan for me in bits and fragments. She does not understand what he intends, but I do. And a plan of my own begins to form.

In order to take my power, Neng must first restore it to me. Since he is a weakling, a fakery, such an influx of power would destroy him. To protect himself, he must end my life at the same moment he absorbs my power. Suseri confides he does not know how to accomplish this without destroying us both.

What Neng does not realize is that I have the knowledge he desires. If I can communicate it to the girl, perhaps we can both be saved.

The seas wail, mourning me. I can hear them pounding against the magician's stronghold. Suseri is preoccupied. It is hard to get her attention in this form—and yet, I must try.

Like a chant, I speak her name. Calling her in my mind. Long ago, her people tended to the dragons, though no one living remembers those days. They spoke to us then—and we spoke to them in return. All my energy is focused on awakening in her that latent talent. Both of our lives depend upon her ability to listen, to hear.

The rain continues. Neng demands wood. She

carries in armload after armload. They land wetly on
the stone floor. Neng waves her away, then draws the
water from the wood and sends it splashing into a
small cauldron balanced over the firepit. He
commands her to light the fire. Then he commands
her to fetch me.

*Suseri. Suseri. Suseri. Suseri. Suseri. Suseri.
Suseri.*

She lifts me with her hands.

*Suseri. Suseri. Suseri. Suseri. Suseri. Suseri.
Suseri.*

She stops in mid-stride and looks about the room,
startled.

*Suseri. Suseri. Suseri. Suseri. Suseri. Suseri.
Suseri.*

Her eyes come to rest on her palm. I wave my
eyestalks encouragingly, still speaking her name. Here
eyes widen. *Can you hear me?* I ask

Yes, she answers.

There is no time for celebration, for awe. *Listen
carefully,* I say. *If you want us both to live.*

With a sneer Neng takes the bowl from her hands.
I am slipping, sliding from center to rim as he tips me
into the boiling cauldron. My last thought is of searing
pain; my last sight is of Suseri, knocking the magician
aside with a smoldering log.

Suddenly, my throat—her throat?—is a bloody
raw wound. The air is filled with screaming. Her

hands—my claws?—are clutching the wizard. He is shouting in rage and pain and fear. My wings beat powerfully, the blazing logs are flung from the firepit as though they were splinters. In a moment, the room is ablaze. We are bursting through the roof. The rain pours down, quenches our terrible thirst, heals the raw wound.

And now, we are over the rocky coast. We release Neng's body and he tumbles, still screaming, to his death on the spires below.

I did as you said. Her voice is my voice. Joyous, exhilaration spills over us. *I drank the water. I drank you.*

And thus my power—

—Is now also mine.

Yes. Ours. We soar away, together.

The Writing
on the Window

Pamela K. Taylor

Nancy Martin skipped down the sidewalk well ahead of her parents, who were enjoying their evening stroll at a more leisurely pace. It had rained that afternoon, and Nancy took extra care to splash in each puddle that had formed in low spots in the concrete. Nancy's parents didn't mind because they remembered how much fun it had been to splash in puddles when they were children, because they liked to think of themselves as the kind of people who would raise a free-spirited, wild child though in fact they were fairly typical modern American parents, and because it gave them time to catch up without having to call out into the cool, dusky, suburban stillness. Other families were out and about—playing a last game of Frisbee before bedtime, taking a quick bike ride before dark, or enjoying an evening stroll like the Martins—but their small noises only accentuated the hush had descended upon the neighborhood along with the impending darkness.

"Ew!" Nancy cried out, breaking the stillness.

"What is it, honey?" her mom asked.

"I stepped on something gross."

"Kids. Spitting their gum out like the whole world was a trash can," her dad said, shaking his head.

"It's not gum." Nancy was sitting on the ground now, looking at a brown smudge on her bare foot. She picked something up off of the concrete and held it for her parents to see.

"Oh, it's just a slug," her dad said.

"Ugh!" her mom said. "Throw it in the street, and wipe your foot on the grass."

Nancy did, pronouncing again that the squashed creature was gross.

Linda Martin sipped her coffee, wiping up a splash of milk Nancy had left on the dinette in her hurry to catch the school bus.

Linda prided herself on being an excellent housewife. Her kitchen was spotless, as were her living room and the dining room; even the family room was neat as a pin. Her windows glistened, she never allowed dust to collect on the bookshelves, the grass was trimmed at least once a week, the flower beds were weed-free, and dinner was on the table at 6 pm every night. Except Wednesdays. And Fridays. Wednesday afternoons, Nancy had ballet class, and Linda couldn't get dinner ready until 6:30. Fridays, it was piano lessons. On Fridays, dinner was at 5:30 Sometimes Linda's husband, Dan, had to heat his up in the microwave, if he got home a bit late.

Linda was a creature of habit. She did the week's grocery shopping on Mondays. Laundry on Tuesdays. Vacuuming on Wednesdays. It made her feel good to have a schedule, as though she weren't just a housewife, but someone who had important tasks at hand. Of course, she told herself regularly, the work a housewife did was vital to the family, and as important as the work of any teacher, or CEO or doctor. But somehow there was always a niggling little voice in her head that said that wasn't true.

Be that as it may, today was Thursday, her morning for yard work, the coffee cup was empty, and it was time to get to work, even if it was sprinkling lightly. She slipped on her raincoat, the green rubber boots and the yellow flowered gardening gloves, and headed to the front door. The flower bed around the mailbox was in desperate need of weeding.

"What the heck!" Linda exclaimed as she opened the door. The walkway to the driveway was dotted with small brownish-grey lumps, dozens of them. "Oh! I hate it! They always come out when it rains."

She retreated into the house. A few moments later, she reappeared with a plastic grocery bag. She plucked slug after slug from the walk, pinching them carefully between thumb and forefinger so as not to squish them and stain her gloves, and threw them into the sack.

"Disgusting things," she said, as she tied the sack and threw it into the garbage can at the end of her drive. Today was garbage day, thank God for small mercies. The thought of all those slugs in her garage, even tied up and in the garbage can gave her the willies.

"You know, we could have done without slugs," Linda said, eyes directed skyward. "Them and mosquitoes. And ants."

Linda squatted beside the mailbox, and began pulling up baby dandelions. At least, there was a whole bagful of slugs that would never eat ugly holes in her begonias.

Saturday mornings were Dan's favorite time of the week. No work, no church, just snuggling with the wife, kid watching cartoons on TV. After a bit, Linda would put the coffee on, toast up some bagels and they'd have breakfast in bed, reading the weekend edition of the local paper.

Until then, he thought, he'd just pull the blanket up around his chin and enjoy the warmth of his wife's back against his chest, and the even, gentle sound of her breathing.

The soft whup-whup of footsteps came down the hall, and across his bedroom floor.

"Daddy?" Dan opened his eyes to see Nancy standing by his side.

"Yes, sweetie," he whispered, trying not to wake Linda.

"What does B-I-G-O-T-S spell?"

Dan sat up, startled. *What the heck?*

"Where'd you hear that word, honey?" he asked, trying to keep the annoyance out of his voice. It must have been the TV; kids shows were really getting out of hand these days. You'd think they could just let kids be innocent for a few years.

"It's on our window."

Dan jumped out of bed and pulled on his robe.

"Show me."

Nancy put her hand in his, led him down the hall to the living room, and pointed at the picture window.

The glass was fogged with condensation. The word "BIGOTS" was scrawled in bold, capital letters in the very middle, with a slash underneath than ran clear across the window.

"Did you see the person who wrote that word?" Dan asked Nancy.

"No, I just saw it when I was getting the remote."

"Thanks for telling me, honey. I'll get mommy to

clean it up. You can go watch your cartoons now."

"But what does it mean?"

"Oh, nothing. It's not a very nice word. Probably some big kids thought it would be a funny joke to write it there so we'd see it when we woke up."

Nancy nodded and then ran down the hall towards the family room. Dan headed back to his nice warm bed. Damn teenagers.

Linda took a bite of Carol's coffee cake. Carol made the best cakes—always light and moist, never dry, and never crumbly. Monday mornings, Linda and the three other stay-at-home moms in their neighborhood got together for coffee and company.

"I swear, we have got to do something about the teenagers in this neighborhood," Joan was saying. She tapped her long, polished nails nervously on the table.

"Did they get you, too?" Nora asked. "My husband was furious. His family was big in the civil rights movement, and when he was in college he was very active in the movement to end discrimination against immigrants."

The drumming nails stopped. "Civil rights?"

"Oh, maybe you're talking about something different. Some kids wrote 'CHAUVINISTS' on our sliding glass door out to the deck, and 'RACISTS on the kitchen window. Clever kids, too; they remembered to write backwards so we could read it from inside. Such a waste of young minds."

"Ours said 'BIGOTS.'" Linda volunteered.

The nails started up again. "Same thing with us. Only ours said 'MURDERERS.' How about you, Carol. Any nasty notes on your windows?"

"No, nothing." There was a moment's silence before Carol added, "Probably couldn't get to my windows through the bushes."

That, Linda thought, was no doubt the truth. Carol believed in a "natural" look for her yard. She had dandelions by the hundreds because she refused to use weed killers; she'd let Virginia creeper grow half way up one wall of her house and hardly ever pruned the shrubbery. She had even encouraged the wild honeysuckle that grew on her back fence, despite the fact that the berries attracted all sorts of beasts.

Nora cleared her throat. Carol's yard care preferences had been an off-limits topic ever since a nasty spat over pesticides had threatened to break up the group.

Joan leaned forward. "The question is how do we catch them? We have to know which teenagers are doing this so we can speak to their parents." She paused dramatically. "Or the police. Vandalism is a crime, you know."

"Oh, come on now, scribbling in the dew can hardly be called vandalism." That was Carol.

"It's not just scribbling in the dew." Joan's voice

was shrill. "The words don't come off easily. You have to scrub them. They must have used soap or grease pencil. And, for your information, graffiti is a form of vandalism. It's punishable with a fine, or sentence of community service. If those boys had to mow a few lawns or wash a few windows, I doubt they'd be writing ugly epithets ever again."

Carol smiled and shook her head. "If you check the penal code, I think you'll find graffiti usually involves paint or some other form of permanent defacement, not something that can be washed off with a bit of soap."

"Carol's got a point," Nora said. She was always trying to stop arguments before they got started. "It takes a little elbow grease, but it does come off."

"Even so. Whoever did it shouldn't get off scot-free."

"Well, why don't you sit up all night and see if you can't catch them," Carol said, a bit tartly.

She has nothing to complain about, Linda thought. *She'd been able to sleep in Saturday morning while the rest of us were scrubbing offensive words off our windows.*

"I think that's just what I'm going to do." The nail drumming had stopped again. "Only I don't have to stay up all night. They had to have done it first thing in the morning, after the dew had settled. Probably on their way to summer football camp, or something. I'll just set the alarm an hour early until they come out again."

Linda climbed up the step ladder clutching a spray bottle of Windex in one hand and a clean rag in the other. This was the third morning that writing had appeared on their picture window. Tuesday's message had been "BROWN IS BEAUTIFUL!" This morning it was, "LIFE, LIBERTY, AND THE PURSUIT OF HAPPINESS FOR ALL!"

She glared at the wispy letters. The first days had been bad enough, but this was almost intolerable. The letters covered very nearly the whole of her window. It would take a good hour to scrub it clean again. She hoped Joan caught the perpetrators soon. Any sympathy she'd felt for Carol's hippie notions had fled. Once they found out who was responsible, Linda planned to extract a good deal of work from them.

"Hey, honey! Come here," Dan called from the front door.

"I'm busy!" Linda answered.

"I know, but this is important."

Linda sighed and climbed down the ladder. "It sure as heck better be." Dan was sitting in front of the TV. A commercial for some household cleaner was playing. "You wanted me to see an ad for Mr. Wipe It?" Linda didn't know whether to thank him or to be insulted.

"No, no. It's coming. On the news."

"Aren't you going to be late for work?"

"They'll have to wait. Shh. Listen."

The morning news announcer, Anita Lareda, a perky brunette, was reading the headlines.

"And now for today's top story, we take you live to our man on the scene, Darnell Walker."

"Thank you, Anita. Tens of thousands of Belmont residents have woken three mornings this past week to find mysterious writing on their windows. Most of the writing appears to be pacifist and civil rights slogans. Police are baffled as to who could have carried out such a large scale effort, and for what purpose."

"It's not just our neighborhood," Dan said, talking over the reporter who was interviewing the Belmont chief of police. "It's the whole city."

Linda motioned for him to hush.

"Reports are coming in from all over the state," the chief was saying. "The same sort of thing is happening everywhere. I don't know any gang has that kind of reach."

"I've heard that similar things are happening in other states as well."

"I heard that too, though of course, our jurisdiction ends at the city limits."

"Do you think the FBI will get involved?"

"They might. 'Course, it's only writing on windows, so they might not, neither."

"Do *you* have any idea who might be responsible?"

"We're thick in the investigation right now. Interviewing people, checking for prints, looking for tracks in the ground below the windows. I have to say, whoever it is, they're pretty smooth operators. So far we haven't got any leads. If we don't find something soon, we're gonna have to put a moratorium on window washing. Destroys the evidence. Home-owner's footprints in the soil, obliterating tracks, fingerprints washed away along with the words. I hope it doesn't come to that, but if we have to, we will. We mean to catch these folks."

"Anita, that about wraps up this story. I'm sure the good folks of Belmont are hoping the authorities catch these folks sooner rather than later."

Dan clicked off the TV.

"That's weird," he said. "I mean, teenagers? That organized? To pull off a stunt like that all through the city? In different states?"

"I'm sure the police will get whoever did this." At least she hoped they would. She was tired of her morning routine being disrupted.

"I gotta get to work, hon." Dan picked up his briefcase and headed for the door. "I'll be home by five thirty."

Linda gave him a kiss and hug.

"Don't worry. If you have to work late, I'll leave

your supper in the microwave. Chili tonight."

"Yummy, yum! Can't wait!"

Linda smiled at her husband's back as he walked down the side walk. It was nice to be appreciated by someone you loved.

"Dan, you've got to come home. Now." Linda sounded on the edge of hysteria.

"What's happened?" Dan asked, fear for Nancy's safety jumping in his heart.

"There are slugs all over the driveway, and the sidewalks too."

"Slugs?" Dan laughed. Linda was usually pretty level-headed, but there were certain things that pushed her buttons, and creepy-crawlies were one of them. "There's nothing to worry about, honey. It's just cause it's been raining so much lately."

"You don't understand. There are hundreds of them. And not just on our driveway. Everywhere."

"I know, they've been out in strength the past couple weeks. Like I said, it's all the rain we've been getting, plus the warm weather. Slug heaven."

"This is different. It's like they're staking out territory or something. They're so thick Nancy couldn't make it home from the bus stop without stepping on hordes of them. I had to go out and carry her halfway."

Dan rolled his eyes. Linda could be so

melodramatic. "It's only three-fifteen, honey. I can't leave now, especially since I came in late this morning."

"Please! They're freaking me out. And pick up some iron sulfate on your way."

"Iron sulfate?"

"I read on the internet iron sulfate will kill them."

"Honey, where am I supposed to get iron sulfate?"

"The hardware store. And if that don't have it, they'll have something else to deal with slugs."

She was serious about this. The window writing had been getting to her. Anything that disrupted the order of her little world sent her out of kilter. Dan rubbed his cheek. He hadn't taken any personal time for three or four months. He should be able to manage a couple hours today. If it would make Linda more comfortable. . . .

"Okay, hon. I'm coming. It'll probably be an hour, by the time I wrap up what I'm doing and stop at the hardware store."

"Oh, thank you, Dan. Thank you!"

Dan finished the paragraph he had been working on, shut down his computer, and straightened his desk a bit before leaving his office.

He stuck his head into the boss's office to make sure it was okay he left a bit early.

"The wife's kinda spooked by all this writing stuff.

Doesn't want to be alone in the house."

"Go ahead, Dan. My wife's been feeling the same way. Sure hope the cops catch the perps so life can get back to normal. See you Monday."

The hardware store parking lot was jam packed.

"Popular place," Dan thought as he walked towards the entrance. Inside everyone seemed to be headed the same direction—garden supplies. A harried looking clerk was standing at the end of the aisle, talking to a red-faced woman.

"I'm sorry, ma'am, we're sold out of metaldehyde and methiocarb, We also have no iron sulfate or iron phosphate. We're recommending salt."

"Salt!" the woman spat.

"Yes, it dehydrates slugs and kills them. Quite quickly, and quite effectively. Just be sure to wash down the area where you've spread it, 'cause it can be hard on the feet of dogs and cats."

Dan hurried down the aisle to a pallet stacked with bags of rock salt, normally sold for deicing driveways. Judging by the size of the crowd, the store would soon be sold out of salt, too. He grabbed two bags and headed to the checkout line. The teenage cashier looked as harried as the clerk.

"Seems like everyone's got an infestation of slugs," Dan said. The cashier just shrugged. "Bumper crop this year. Too much rain, and nice warm summer nights."

"It's good for business." The cashier looked like she'd just as soon business were bad. "Good luck," she said as he walked away, one bag of salt under each arm.

As he drove home, he couldn't help but notice every driveway, every sidewalk was littered with slugs.

He pulled into his own drive with a sick feeling in his stomach, imagining all those slug bodies being crushed under his wheels. It would be a slimy mess. Hopefully the rain would wash most of it away.

Linda met him at the door.

"Did you get it?" she asked.

"In the trunk," he told her. She didn't need to know it was only salt. So long as it killed the slugs, she'd be happy.

"They really need to do something about this," Linda said. "Spray for them or something, like they do with mosquitoes."

"They sure seem to be out in force today," Dan agreed. He wondered if it was just an especially good summer for slugs, or if they sensed something wrong, like an earthquake coming, or a tornado.

"I'll wait for you inside." Linda shuddered and let the door close behind her with a slam.

Dan hauled one of the bags out of the trunk and began sprinkling salt over the slugs. They curled into balls, writhing, a silent testimony to agony. A bad taste rose in Dan's throat.

"I can't do this," he said aloud. He put the salt back in the car, and went to get the snow shovel. He couldn't kill them, not so many of them at once, not in such a barbaric way.

There was a hedge between their house and the neighbors to the west. He scooped the slugs off the driveway and dumped them in the mulch under the hedge.

Linda wouldn't be any the wiser, and his conscience would be a lot cleaner.

Saturday morning, Dan lay in bed, unable to go back to sleep. Would there be any new messages on the windows? Another onslaught of slugs? He was pretty sure they would have crawled out of the mulch overnight, and that his driveway would be covered again.

At last he got out of bed, and slipped on his robe. No point lying there if he couldn't sleep. He walked into the living room.

"SLIME IS OF THE ESSENCE." was scrawled in the middle of the window. What the hell was that supposed to mean? Some teenage wisecrack, inspired by the overabundance of slugs, no doubt.

Dan sighed and headed to kitchen. He needed coffee. Sleep had been slow coming the night before. He hadn't been able to stop thinking of tortured slugs thrashing around on his driveway.

On the window over the sink were the words, "SLUG POWER!"

"Oh great," he thought. More work for Linda. She was going to be delighted.

While the coffee brewed, he walked around the house. Seven windows had words written on them:

"WITHOUT SLUGS WHERE WOULD YOUR WASTE GO?"

"WE'RE NOT SLIMY, WE'RE MOIST!"

"STOP STEREOTYPING SLUGS!"

"HUG A SLUG TODAY!"

"SLUGS MAKE THE WORLD GO ROUND."

This was getting out of hand. If he got a hold of the kids who were responsible for this, Dan swore he'd wring a few necks. He ran a hand over his eyes, poured a cup of coffee and flipped on the TV. A local news magazine show was on. Seattle-AM, or something like that. Three men and a woman sat on a pair of loveseats, chatting about current events.

"Grant, this is not a localized phenomenon," the earnest-faced host, Jack Nelson, was saying. "We're getting reports from all over the nation. The South, the Pacific Northwest, New England—any place with a relatively humid, warm climate—we're all facing an infestation of slugs."

"Yes, Jack, and it's bad enough that's even it's caught the attention of the mysterious window writers," Grant Ballard, who was identified as belonging to the Seattle Horticulturalist Society, replied.

The third man, one Brian Neelson fron AAA PestAway, spoke up. "Got to admit, they sure do have a sense of humor. 'Slugs of the World Unite!' 'Justice for Slugs!' 'Stop Killing my Brothers!' And my personal favorite, 'Slugs for Peaceful Coexistence!'"

"*My* favorite is this one from Pennsylvania. . . ." Jack rifled through his papers and read aloud "'Slugs are not gross, disgusting, ugly, or loathsome; they are a necessary and beautiful part of the ecosystem, and just as much a part of God's creation as any other creature. Grow up! Deal with your irrational fears! Embrace the slug!'"

Grant chuckled. One of those fake TV announcer chuckles. "That one must have covered an entire display window."

"Quite a philosopher." Brian offered up his own fake chuckle. "Or a biologist perhaps."

"Funny you should mention that, Brian. Sitting next you is Dr. Renee Whitaker, a pre-eminent biologist whose specialty is the study of slugs. Dr. Whitaker, thank you for joining us. So what you think about this sudden overabundance of slugs?"

"Actually, it's a bit baffling. The conditions across much of their range have been favorable, but not to such a degree as to warrant the exponential jump we've seen this year."

"In other words, you don't know why there are so many slugs this year."

"We suspect that it isn't so much a growth in the population, but a change in normal behavior patterns. Rather than remaining in the garden, or beneath the leaf litter, they're coming out into the open."

"Sunbathing?" Jack quipped, with an arch flip of the wrist.

Dr. Whitaker gave him a frosty look. "Not at all. We think, however, that it might have something to do with global warming and climate change. Evening temperatures not sinking as low, greater humidity in the regions that slugs populate."

Jack nodded vaguely, clearly uninterested in environmental issues.

"What do you make of the window greetings this morning?"

"Well, I certainly agree with whoever has been writing the messages. Slugs play a very important role in our eco-system. They are essential in the decomposition of dead plant and animal matter. They serve as a prey species for a large number of animals— toads, mice, snakes, certain species of birds, even other slugs. Really, I find the overwhelming revulsion towards slugs to be completely nonsensical. They should be valued for the vital work they do."

"Slimy, cold, clammy, oozy things. Don't slugs make you shudder? Even a little."

"Not at all. Men who bomb cities full of civilians so we can take the oil from under their soil. Men who shoot their wives and girlfriends out of jealousy or the need to control. Men who mindlessly kill defenseless gastropods because of some primal, instinctive reaction. That makes me shudder. Small, defenseless creatures who do the world's dirty work. Not at all."

"Well, guess that's clear enough." For once Jack seemed to be at a loss for words.

"Did you know that Dr. Alan Gelperin, a neurobiologist at UPenn, has discovered that on tests of memory and logic, slugs have results comparable to rats, pigeons, and undergraduate students?"

"Are you saying we should send slugs to college?"

"No, but neither should we hate them simply because they have damp skins, or because they provide their own lubrication for reduced friction travel, or because they lack a bony skeleton such as ours."

"Well, thank you, Dr. Whitaker. It's been a pleasure talking with you," Jack said, with a toothy grin that looked as fake as his laugh sounded. "When we get back, the latest developments on the window writers. We have a witness who claims the words aren't written by humans at all. According to him, the slugs are doing it!"

Dan clicked the TV off and checked over his

shoulder. That was the last thing Linda needed to hear. She was already going a bit haywire. Maybe he'd take her into the city. A nice outing would take her mind off the stress of the week. The Children's Museum, he thought, would do the trick nicely. Nancy loved the children's museum. Course, if he wanted Linda to go, he'd better get the windows cleaned up before she could see the mess all over them. She wouldn't leave the house until every last mark was gone.

Joan's cake wasn't as good as Carol's but it was delectable. Linda felt as though she could sit in this big, overstuffed chair sipping coffee and nibbling cake for the rest of her life. And if she couldn't care less if she never again washed a window.

"I don't understand why they're not all over your place," Joan whined. "I've put out metaldehyde three times, and each time it seems like there's even more the next day. I don't know where they're coming from."

"Maybe if you'd stop killing them, they'd leave you alone," Carol said. "I've never killed a slug in my life, and they aren't bothering me."

"Don't be ridiculous. Slugs can't think."

Carol pursed her lips, but didn't say anything.

"Maybe it's worth a try," Nora said. "The slugs over here sure seem to be going about their ordinary lives rather than hanging out on the driveway and the sidewalks."

"I think it's those teenagers. They've got a supply somewhere and each night they dump more on our driveways."

"Oh, come off it, Joan! This is going on across half the nation. You don't think any teenagers could pull off that kind of stunt, do you?"

"More than I think a bunch of slugs could."

Carol was silent again.

"What? You believe those nuts who claim that the slugs are writing those messages themselves, and that they're holding sit-ins on all our driveways and sidewalks?"

Carol looked like she was going to hold her tongue, but at last she burst out.

"Have you caught the teenagers yet? I thought you were going to lie in wait for them."

Joan shifted in her seat. "No, I haven't caught them yet. But I will. I will. And I can guarantee you, it isn't any slug doing this."

Linda usually stayed out of the way when Carol and Joan got into it, but this time she had to speak up. "Dan's been killing them since Friday, and we're getting fewer and fewer each day. It's almost back to normal."

Carol shrugged, and turned away. "I don't know," she said, looking out the window. "I just think we ought to live and let live. That's the way God intended the world to be. None of this killing insects and animals just because they happen to eat the same things we do. There's plenty to go around."

"Great," Joan retorted. "I'll bring my slugs over here, so you live in harmony with them."

Carol looked her steadily in the eye.

"That'd be better than killing them wholesale. Anything's better than genocide."

"Bye, hon, see you at six," Dan called to his wife as he headed towards the garage.

"Okay, sweetie. Grilled salmon and asparagus with hollandaise tonight."

"Oh, man," Dan groaned. "I may have to come home early!"

Linda laughed. "Oh, scoot! It won't be done yet if you get home early."

Dan heaved a sigh of relief as he got into his car. It was great to have his wife back. Two weeks without any new messages on the windows had made a huge difference in her mood. No new messages, and no slug infestation. Their numbers had started tapering off the day he bought the salt, and three days later they had practically disappeared.

Of course, not everyone was so lucky. Some houses were practically besieged by the creatures. Just this morning, the news had shown one of his own neighbors—the wife was a friend of Linda's—their home was so thick with slugs you couldn't even see what color of the siding. The drive was knee-deep in them. The couple was frantic. They had tried all the pesticides, salt, beer traps, Diatomaceous earth, strips of copper. They'd even lit a bonfire in the middle of their driveway. All to no avail. The next day, the slugs were back, thicker than before.

"I don't know why they're picking on us," the woman had complained. "It should be pretty clear by now, we don't want them here. We hate them!"

"If it doesn't stop soon," the man said, "We're going to move to New Mexico. No slugs in the desert."

Might as well get that salt out the trunk, he thought. He'd left it hidden in the back of his car all this time. He'd been afraid that if he moved it to one of the storage shelves in the garage Linda might find out he hadn't had the guts to use it and work herself into a panic that the slugs would be back. Enough time had passed now, though, that she wouldn't worry. She might tease him a bit about being a softy, but he could stand that.

He walked around to the back of his car, and turned the key in the lock, thinking that it had proven convenient that he'd never made a spare for Linda.

He reached for the bags of salt, and was surprised to see sitting not far from them, a single slug. It was long, sleek, and fat. Its back was a rich tan dappled with dark brown spots. It was actually beautiful in its own way—a granddaddy leopard of slugs. As he watched, the slug began to climb up the side of the trunk towards him. Dan swallowed, but kept watching the creature. It moved faster than he would have expected. Before long it had reached the flat flange at the back of the trunk.

"I should pick him up," Dan thought, "Otherwise I'll have to wash his slime off the back of my car."

That was when he noticed that the snail wasn't headed for the edge of the car, as he'd thought, but was making an erratic pattern on the back of his car.

No, Dan corrected himself, not erratic. It spelled out a word. T-H-A-N-K-S.

Dan gently picked up the slug, and deposited it under the hedge. Then he wiped the slime trail off the back of his car. There was no way he was going to let Linda see that.

Bubblers Anonymous

Roger L. Johnson

It was a typical rainy Spring morning in Port Orchard, Washington. Doctor Maynard S. Lugger stood at his office window looking out on the Sinclair Inlet and the Puget Sound Naval Shipyards. To the west a quarter mile stood three mothballed aircraft carriers; gray warriors from a time far in the past. His eyes dropped to Bay Street where groups of tourists—mostly tortoises—scampered about with dizzying speed from one knick-knack store to another.

The doctor turned about to his desk where a stack of newspaper articles lay paper clipped together. He scanned the first. The banner headline read: BUBBLERS ANONYMOUS: A GREAT SUCCESS! The support group had been the doctor's brainchild and personal project to counter the devastating effects of the recent rash of gastropod salt abuse and deaths in surrounding counties. To date, he had referred forty-five young slugs and snails to the program, reducing the recidivism rate from 82% down to an all-time low of 32%. He removed the paper clip and read:

> With several locations on the Kitsap Peninsula from Gig Harbor to Silverdale, Doctor Lugger's very successful Bubblers Anonymous intervention program might be a snail and slug's last-ditch hope for a salt free life of normalcy. Herds of these precious gastropods—most of them very young—have been decimated by the ravages of salt abuse. Recent studies throughout the Pacific Northwest have uncovered alarming statistics indicating that nearly half of all young slugs who are still in their first year of life have tried this deadly substance at least once. By an act of the Washington State Legislature, Doctor Lugger's Bubblers Anonymous was created and funded by a $5 million dollar grant from the recently built Herbert S. Nail Desalinization Plant near Port

Townsend. The youth of
Washington have been given a
second chance—a chance to 'kick
the salt habit' and return to a
normal life. It is both sad and
ironic that what was a slug's
greatest enemy—salt—has now
become an object of commerce;
exposing the sticky underbelly of
the drug cartel and. . . .

The doctor looked at the clock and pulled a court
file from his inbox. The name on the cover was Jerold
S. Nail. He didn't like it that a full twenty percent of
the cases referred to him by District Court Judge
Myrna Slyme were *pro-bono*, but in the present state
of affairs, that was one of the hoops a leading therapist
had to jump through to remain in good standing with
the courts.

There was a commotion outside in the reception
area. The doctor slid to the door, pushed it open just
enough to allow a single antennae to snake through
the opening far enough to see what was the matter.
Two uniformed slugs who were obviously too big for
their uniforms had young Jerold trussed between
them. He was typical of the youth who were leaving
their salt-stained tracks through the Juvenile Court
system and were filling the jails. Baggy clothes that

barely clung to his sticky skin and at least a dozen piercings of various parts of his long body identified the youth as a trouble-maker. He was a light yellow color—a little lighter than the doctor—with just the beginnings of his adult markings along his back. The spots looked more like garish tattoos than the usual liver spots of his particular breed. One of the officers handed a court document to the receptionist while the other pushed the young slug down into one of the plastic chairs.

"I'll see if Doctor Lugger is ready for you, Mr.—?" She waited for him to tell her, but the young slug wouldn't look up. "I didn't catch your name, young man."

"It's Nail," said the officer who was holding the young gastropod down in the chair. "Jerold, S."

The receptionist pushed the intercom. "Doctor Lugger, there's a young slug here from," she looked up at the officers, "the court. Are you ready for him?"

The doctor closed the door and slid back to his desk. He pushed the button. "Yes, show him in."

The officer pulled Jerold up by his baggy shirt and pushed him to the door. "You want for me to take you all the way in and stick you to the couch, or are you gonna cooperate with somebody for a change?" Th

Jerold looked up at the slug and gave him a passive look. "Whatever."

"Look, you little sorry excuse for a snail, it's either

you be nice and talk with the doctor or you go to Ortho Prison right now!"

Jerold gave the officer a barely noticeable shrug and slid to the door. "Yeah! I'll talk with the doctor, if that's what it's gonna take to get you off my case."

Doctor Lugger met Jerold at the door and ushered him inside. "There!" he said, pointing at the plastic couch. The doctor slid to his desk and picked up the newspaper article. "You're his grandson, aren't you?"

Jerold stopped in front of the window and looked out on the Puget Sound. "You didn't think I got referred to you because you're such a great psychiatrist, did you?"

"Shall we begin?"

Jerold slid to the couch but stopped. He looked up at the doctor. "What's the matter? What are you looking at?"

Doctor Lugger looked down at Jerold's track across the polished hardwood floor. He looked up at the youth. "That color. When was the last time you bubbled?"

Jerold turned about. "Who told you I—" He fell silent, knowing he had already said far too much. "Who said I've *ever* bubbled?"

"Look," said the doctor, pointing down at the distinctive tracks. "Only slugs and snails who do salt leave that color."

Jerold slithered up onto the couch and turned around so he could see the doctor. "So, what am I supposed to do here so you'll tell them to let me go home?"

"Is that all you want—to go home? What about what the officer said? What about Ortho Prison? They tell me you're looking at three to five years."

"What would you want, Doc, if you were in my tracks?"

"I'd want to have clean tracks," Doctor Lugger said, giving the foul slime a glance. "That would be where I'd start. Then I'd want to go home to my family and stop hurting them. That would be a wonderful beginning."

"Have you ever bubbled, Doc? Have you ever snorted salt?"

"I ask the questions here, Jerold, not you."

"It's a fair question isn't it?"

The doctor thought for a moment. He wasn't sure what approach would get through to this troubled young gastropod. He could play the classic angry father, but that seldom worked with the kind of young slug that sat before him. Then there was the coach—give him lots of support and point him to a glorious horizon—but he had the distinct feeling that Jerold was beyond having that kind of smoke blown up his skirt. The empathetic fellow sufferer would be best, and since he had already asked the key question, the doctor changed his pace.

"Well," asked Jerold with a slight movement of his head, "have you?"

"I suppose we all experimented a little when we were young, but most of us realized early on that the damage salt would do to our bodies—and to the people who care for us—was not worth the cheap rush we got from bubbling."

"You didn't answer my question, Doc. Have you ever abused salt? Have you ever bubbled?"

"Once, but it was so awful I never went near the stuff again."

"At least you know something about it, that's a hell of a lot more than that judge and those pushy cops out there."

The doctor looked at Jerold's chart. "I see that you've been enrolled in Bubblers Anonymous three different times and have always dropped out." He looked up at Jerold. "Why? What happened?"

"They're all losers, that's why!"

"But it's a good program. Everybody wants to help you."

"I'll go to jail before I go back to all that mental masturbation."

"Are you talking about Bubblers Anonymous or me?"

"Both!" Jerold looked up, this time with fire in his eyes. "Isn't that what you do? Screw with our brains?"

"No—"

"—That's why I'm here, isn't it?"

The doctor held up the file. "Why don't we talk about how you got started. How did it happen?"

"Like most everybody, I guess."

"Beer?"

Jerold nodded.

"When was that?"

"In the fall, just after I found out I wasn't a snail."

"Huh!" said the doctor with a chuckle. "That's when I tried salt too. I guess it's an important day for all of us."

"I only wanted to do beer. It gave me a great rush." Jerold chuckled.

"What?"

"Oh, that word—rush. Kind of antithetical for *our* kind."

The doctor nodded. "Let's get back to the salt—the first time."

"Yeah. There was salt—some of my best friends were snorting lines over an inch long and then bubbling for an hour. I didn't like the looks of it—watching them rolling up into little balls and getting all covered with spit bubbles—so I passed up their offer. They made fun of me. They called me a snail."

"How did you feel about that—being called a snail?"

"It hurt."

"Bad enough to succumb to peer pressure?"

Jerold gave a shrug.

"So. What changed?"

"You mean, how did I move up to the hard stuff?" The doctor nodded.

"It was last month, just after the first thaw. Some of us got together to celebrate and out came the beer, like usual. We were all sipping, telling snail jokes—"

The doctor cleared his throat and looked up from his pad of paper. "You could get in a lot of trouble for that."

"What?" Jerold made a sarcastic face. "Telling *snail* jokes?"

"It's classed as a hate crime to make fun of our shelled cousins."

"Cousins, my slippery ass!" Jerold spat. "They're just snails—duck food—not worth their slime!"

"You could have been born a snail, Jerold. Did you ever think of that?"

"I wasn't though, was I? And that's why I drank the beer. We were celebrating."

"What happened next."

"You think it's easy being my age, don't you?"

"I don't want to argue with you, Jerold. I just want to know what happened. Where'd the salt come from?"

Jerold gave a huff, pulled his tentacles in for a moment and then allowed them to poke back out. "We were all sipping the beer, telling the jokes and feeling the rush. We don't know who did it, but somebody dumped in a full packet of salt. One of us should have noticed when the head formed on the top of the beer, but by then, we were all too wasted."

"So." The doctor wrote something on his pad. "So, it was never your *intention* to ingest the salt?"

"None of us knew until it was too late."

"What happened next?"

"Oh, man! It was like those fireworks everybody told us about!" An involuntary shiver crept up Jerold's body and several bubbles formed at the corners of his mouth. "Everything went kind of crazy for a couple of minutes and then all these bubbles started coming from our mouths. There was a lot of yelling and gagging, and then we all rolled into balls and the lights went out. I don't know how long we lay there like that, but when we finally started waking up, we were changed."

"How? What do you mean, you were changed?"

"All those stories our teachers and parents told us; how salt would kill us or make us go crazy."

"But those stories are—"

"It didn't kill us, Doc!"

The doctor recoiled at the smell of fresh salt on the youth's breath.

"It was all a lie!"

"So, how did it change you?"

"Two ways." Jerold smiled the way only young slugs could smile. "First—like I said—we found out our parents and teachers were liars."

The doctor frowned. "What was the second thing that changed?"

"We tasted the forbidden fruit and we found out how good it was."

The doctor gave a defeated huff. He had never come up against such an able foe. Now it was personal. Jerold might end up dead in a few days from a salt overdose. If it happened, it was only a statistic on a chart and statistics could be manipulated. But the doctor was determined. He wouldn't the impetuous youth to maintain the upper hand.

"I didn't do any of the expensive stuff—iodized or Sea Salt—for several months."

"Oh?"

Jerold gave a chuckle. "You know about salt substitutes, right?"

"Yes. I know about them."

"We tried them all, but they didn't give us that same rush—that same burn that the hard stuff gave us. Mrs. Salt just made our breath smell funny." Jerold laughed.

"Where did it come from—the salt?"

Jerold stopped laughing. He looked at the doctor.

"What's the matter, Jerold? What are you looking for?"

"Your shell! Where is it?"

"I'm a slug, Jerold, just like you."

"But you're acting like a snail, Doctor Lugger. You can't be *this* stupid an be a slug!"

The doctor squirmed in his slick chair.

"You're just like the rest, aren't you?"

"What?"

"You don't see anything, you don't hear anything and you don't say anything. It's all politics—the slugs telling us lies and the snails swearing to it."

"What are you talking about? What lies?"

"The lies from the slugs down in Olympia. The slugs that control the state. The snails who run the newspapers, television and radio stations."

"I don't know what you're talking about, Jerold. What lies?"

Jerold gave the doctor another one of his looks. "You're being straight with me, aren't you?" When the doctor still looked puzzled, Jerold shook his head and said, "You really don't know, do you?"

"Tell me, Jerold. What are they lying about?"

"My grandfather's desalinization plant up at Port Townsend. Thousands of gallons of fresh water. What do you think happens to all that leftover salt? Do you think its saved to spread on icy roads?"

"I always assumed it was—" The doctor stopped. He shook his head.

"One question first," said Jerold, leaning forward.

"What?"

"Can you tell the police or the judge anything I tell you in this room?"

"No," said the doctor, shaking his head, "it's against the law. What we talk about in this room is protected, confidential."

Jerold looked at the doctor for what seemed to be a full minute. Finally, he took a deep breath. "The Kitsap Salt Cartel. We have our supply lines and we make payoffs whenever and wherever we to keep the salt flowing. Our network is deep and well established. We have dealers and pushers. We have judges, attorneys and police officers on our payroll. We get all the salt we want—all the salt we need. Everybody is getting rich, and everybody is getting high."

The doctor was in shock. He couldn't move.

"You've tried it more than that one time! You know how great it is! You've had the rush, and you keep coming back, just like all the rest of us!"

"No. I—" The doctor tried to shake his head, but it wouldn't move.

"I know about your habit, Doctor Lugger."

"But how—"

"Because I'm three steps away in your upstream. The salt you sniffed yesterday in the privacy of your hillside mansion passed through my hands an hour before you bought it." Jerold laughed so loud that the secretary slid to the door to make sure everything was all right. The doctor waved her away.

He turned back to the young slug. "What's so funny?"

"The irony of it all. Think about it, Doctor Lugger, You're profit and I'm overhead."

The doctor considered where the conversation had gone. Bubbles started coming from his mouth—bubbles of fear. "You won't get away with—"

"I already have, Doctor, and that's why I'm here."

"What are you talking about?"

"We've been watching you."

The bubbling increased. Not the kind of bubbling you get from salt, but the kind that comes from deep primeval fear. The doctor slid from his chair and backed toward the corner. He spit some of the bubbles away. "What do you want from me?"

"Your cooperation, Doctor Lugger. I want to put you on our payroll."

"*Your* payroll? Are you crazy?"

"Isn't that why I'm here?" Jerold said with another laugh. "Aren't you trying to find out whether or not I'm crazy?"

Lugger wasn't listening. "I could be sent to Ortho Prison," he mumbled. "I'd lose my license. . . ."

Jerold was still talking. ". . . It would be like Christmas in April."

The doctor spit away the new bubbles that had collected around his mouth, slid to the door, and pushed it open. The two police officers stood and slid forward. He looked back in at Jerold. The youth gave him a cold stare.

"Everything alright, Doc?" asked the larger of the two, looking up at the clock. "You still have twenty minutes with our prisoner."

"I need you inside," he said.

Jerold was up. He had moved to the window. The track across the carpet was now showing signs of fear.

The two officers slid into the office. They recognized the fear in Jerold's track. They looked at the doctor and the larger one spoke. "What is it, Doc?"

"Since the judge's order allows me to decide whether Kitsap County will be best served by Jerold Nail going to Ortho Prison or working in a recovery and rehabilitation program of my design . . . ." The doctor looked across at Jerold. The youth was obviously scared, but he was standing his ground.

"I have decided that Jerold S. Nail should continue with his therapy and group intervention sessions at Bubblers Anonymous. We have made terrific progress in even this short session, and I can assure you, and Judge Slyme, that within six months, our young friend will be completely healed of his salt addiction and will return to society, a full and functioning slug."

The officers looked from Jerold to the doctor. The larger one pulled a sheet of paper from his vest. "Just sign at the bottom then and he's all yours."

A few minutes later, the two police officers were gonne. Jerold looked out on the Puget Sound. When he heard the door close, he turned around. He looked expectantly at Dr. Ludder, waiting for his terms.

"I want a retainer of $10,000 in cash a month and another $10,000 bonus in cash every time I release one of your associates. I also want all the free salt I can use."

"It's a deal!" Jerold grinned, then laughed loudly.

"What's so funny?"

Jerold shook his head. Still laughing, he slid to the door and pushed it open. The receptionist's area was empty. He pushed the button for the elevator. "You really are a snail, doctor. You could've had double that. And more." The elevator arrived. Jerold slid into it. His laughter lingered long after the doors had closed.

The Familiar

Kelly Madden

Jennifer Millicent Treebottoms the Third, Jenny to her friends, sat thoughtfully on a bench at the edge of her garden. It was her thinking seat, a place she came to ruminate over life's problems. She smiled. Not that she had that many. The last hundred years had been good ones. No matter what the oldsters said, it was a good time to be young and alive. She stretched her arms high over her head. It was good to be filled with magic. Jenny sighed contentedly. No, she wouldn't give up her life as a witch for anything.

A slight frown creased her lovely features. There was, she considered, that one thing. The thing she had dreaded. The thing she had avoided. As her mother, several Aunties, and many other senior females had told her, it was time. Past time. Jenny gazed thoughtfully over her gardens. The moonlight glinted off her perfectly aligned plantings; pale blossoms of many varieties swayed in the light breeze sending their sweet perfumes as if a gift to their tender.

Jenny left her bench and walked slowly through her flowers, allowing feathery foliage to caress her fingers. What if it hurt her garden? She knew size, as any other descriptor, could not be requested. You got what you got. She thought of her perfectly quaint cottage: knickknacks, paintings, and furnishings arranged just so. What if it demanded to live inside with her? She shuddered. What if it . . . left droppings inside?

Jenny took a deep breath, steadying herself. Perhaps it wouldn't be so bad. Maybe it would even be cute. But then, even the nicest ones could be a bother. Jenny thought of walking through Paris streets in the springtime, enjoying coffee in Rio, and shopping in the smoky Kasbah markets. She would never be free to come and go again.

Jenny balled her fists, but quickly forced herself to release her anger. It was the way of things, and that was that. She gazed up at the moon; its twin sickle points curved gently upwards.

It was time to assume her adult responsibilities.

Jenny raised her arms again to the night sky, closed her eyes, and said the incantation:

Fur and tooth or fin and scale
Wings aloft or trailing tail
Companion come I beg of thee
Together we forever be.

Jenny swallowed, her eyes squeezed shut. She listened carefully but her garden was silent. She cautiously opened one eye, then another, but she saw nothing. Her shoulders sank with relief. At least it wasn't an elephant, or something huge. Her best friend had gotten a white rhino. And while impressive, it took constant work to keep the animal in food. She grimaced. And to clean its stall. Jenny turned around slowly. Nothing behind her either. Her eyes swept the night sky thinking maybe what-ever-it-was might fly to her, but again she was disappointed. Her heart started to beat faster. Jenny knew her powers would begin to fade if her companion did not arrive and while it was not common, it *had* happened. She fluffed the flower heads and shook out a few night moths, but they fluttered away. It wasn't to be a moth or butterfly either, she thought sadly.

Just as she was starting to become extremely concerned, she felt the slightest flutter inside her head. Not words really, but the faintest awareness like a feather drawn across the skin. Jenny shivered in delight. *Yes.* This was how it had been described to her. She knew the link would become stronger over time, and eventually she and her companion would be able to speak with one another.

Jenny whirled around. Where was her companion, her friend for life, her Familiar? She felt the feathery caress again. It was here, and it was close. She bent down to the ground and looked down the stone pathway, but still saw nothing.

Where are you? she cried internally.

Down.

Jenny started at the first word, and smiled. She parted the soft grasses. It must be small. That was good. She brightened. Maybe a sweet garden mouse or perhaps a young creature. A baby fox, perhaps. Jenny pushed aside the green fronds faster and faster. Where was it?

Careful.

Jenny jumped again, but did slow down. She didn't want to hurt it, after all. Suddenly she felt something. Something wet. She frowned and almost flicked it away when she heard the voice again.

Here.

Jenny felt her heart sink to her toes as she slowly lifted her fingers.

It was a slug.

Small, moist, and glistening in the light, it was the most disgusting thing she had ever seen. Even though Jenny was an accomplished gardener, she always wore gloves so as not to have to touch anything slimy and squashy. She made herself look down at her hand. It seemed to be staring at her from eyes perched high on twin stalks.

Um, hello, Jenny thought tentatively.

Greetings, it thought to her.

Jenny watched as the delicate eyestalks twitched back and forth. Studying her. She shuddered, and forced herself not to hold her hand away from her. What was she supposed to do with a slug?

She took a deep calming breath. It was, after all, her Familiar. Her companion. She swallowed. For life. She considered what she would have done for a furry animal.

Would you like something to eat? A place to rest?

Both would be nice, thank you.

Jenny walked slowly towards her cottage, her hand kept at a stiff ninety degree angle. She didn't want to lose it in the tall foliage, and she certainly didn't want to dump it accidentally on her person.

Jenny pushed the door open with her free hand and glanced around the room. She looked down at the slug, its soft body quivering in the slight breeze she had made from walking. She needed something smooth. She grimaced. And moist.

Jenny quickly located a small porcelain bowl from the kitchen and gently placed the slug inside. She smiled slightly as she perceived a wave of pleasure from it as it slipped inside. She placed a small basin of water and a bit of lettuce nearby. The slug showed its appreciation by devouring a leaf.

Delicious. My thanks.

You're welcome, Jenny thought to it, a bit awkwardly.

Jenny felt a wave of something that felt like humor waft towards her.

I'm not what you expected.

Jenny swallowed. How had it known? *Well. . . .*

That's all right. I understand.

No. I don't mean, what I really mean is, you're my Familiar, and. . . .

Don't worry about it. You've already been more than kind. We'll get used to one another.

Jenny suddenly saw herself from the slug's perspective: A huge giantess with wide, glassy eyes. She smiled. She hadn't thought that the slug might find *her* repulsive.

Jennifer Millicent Treebottoms the Third, Jenny to my friends, she thought to it, holding out her finger.

Lypedia, Ly to my friends, the slug replied, tipping its eyes to touch her finger gently.

The slug Ly curled up at the back of the bowl, and Jenny supposed it meant to rest. She sank down slowly onto a sofa opposite her new Familiar.

Well, she thought, that was that. There was no use getting upset, and Ly seemed nice enough. She knew that some of her friends had received companions that were decidedly cranky, even mean. Ly was very polite. The clock chimed softly, and with the sound Jenny's heart sank as she remembered something she had forgotten.

She leaned her head back and almost started to cry. The dance. Tonight. The biggest ball of the year. The coming out event where new Familiars were introduced. She sniffed quietly. She'd have to show Ly to her friends. And all the others who were definitely *not* her friends. She felt a tear leak out of the corner of one eye and wiped it away. Arlia and her raven. It had pecked a few people, but it was beautiful. Malina and her impressive wolf. And then there was Carnella and her cat. Her *cat*. Jenny scowled. It was enough that Carnella was the most beautiful witch around, but no, she also had to have the most gorgeous Familiar Jenny had ever seen. Carnella, her cat, and her entourage of silly, cruel girls. Jenny knew what they would say about her new companion.

Her eyes flicked to the bowl and she felt a rush of guilt. Jenny knew she shouldn't feel this way, but she couldn't help it. She sighed heavily, but managed to push aside her sad thoughts. She spent the rest of the night tidying up her home, stopping every now and then to check on Ly who seemed content. It did not speak further to her. Jenny went to bed as dawn sneaked over the horizon and was soon asleep.

Jenny awoke to the whirring of cicadas' evening song and knew it was time to get ready for the dance. She drew on a gown soft as cobwebs and piled her hair atop her head. Slowly Jenny approached her Familiar. How was she to carry it? She suppressed a shudder. In her hand?

She cleared her throat, and was rewarded with twin eyestalks peeking over the edge of the bowl.

Time for the dance?

How did you—? Never mind. Yes. It's time.

I was thinking. I need some kind of portable home. Something smooth and small. Jenny watched as it tilted its head to one side. *A necklace perhaps.*

Jenny smiled and walked to her jewel chest. She removed a delicate silver chain on which was strung a gleaming, whorled shell. She had found it by the sea and had polished it until it shone. She brought it to Ly.

Perfect.

The slug wriggled inside and Jenny carefully looped it around her neck. She didn't much want the slug to touch her skin.

Jenny noted the slanting light through the window; she'd need to hurry now to make it on time. Luckily the ball was not far as the broomstick flew, and soon Jenny was slipping silently through the night sky.

She circled the old Victorian house once before landing. The transplanted house was always lovely, but tonight, festooned with pale paper lanterns, it looked even more enchanted. She alighted gently on the front lawn and a few people waved at her. She smiled but proceeded directly inside. Jenny wanted to be safely ensconced before Carnella made her grand appearance.

Carnella and her *cat*.

Jenny frowned. It was a shoe-in who would win the Best Familiar Award. Not only was the animal beautiful, but Jenny had also heard through the grapevine that it was very powerful. And as if her thoughts had called her nemesis to her, Jenny heard the bright laughter of Carnella and her ever-present entourage.

Jenny retreated to a small island of over-stuffed chairs and sank down low, but Carnella spied her nonetheless. As she strode towards her, Jenny admitted that Carnella did look stunning: Her white-blond hair was interwoven with pearls and sparkling stones, and a form-fitting dress that matched the silvery fur of the cat draped around her shoulders was a breathtaking sight.

"Jennifer, what a lovely dress. It looks so pretty on you. *Every* time you wear it."

Jenny clamped her teeth shut, and smiled tightly.

"Thank you, Carnella. You look nice too."

Carnella smiled. "So . . . where is it? I've been dying to know."

Jenny took a deep breath. This was it. She touched her necklace. "Here."

Carnella frowned and bent forward. As she did so, two eyestalks looked out.

"Ick! What's that?"

"A slug."

"Disgusting! How long will it be that way? When will it have, you know, wings?"

Jenny almost laughed despite her embarrassment. Carnella was cunning, but she could be rather dumb. "Ly is not a caterpillar."

Carnella looked shocked, then a sly smile crossed her beautiful features. "You mean . . . the thing will *always* be like this?"

Jenny squared her shoulders. "Yes."

Carnella and her entourage hooted with laughter. Jenny stood tall and stared each of them in the eyes, including Carnella, who finally backed away uncomfortably.

"Well. I guess I don't have anything to worry about," she said airily, stroking her cat and disappearing into the gathering crowd.

Jenny sank back into her chair. It had been as bad as she had imagined, but it was over. *Why*, she wondered for the millionth time, *did Carnella seem to enjoy picking on her?*

She's jealous.

Jenny sat straight up in her chair. *Carnella? No way.*

She's envious of everything about you. Your beauty, your talent, your confidence.

Jenny shook her head. *But she has everything! Like that ca—*

Jenny stopped herself. She didn't want Ly to think she was disappointed with having a slug for a Familiar.

Jenny . . . about that cat . . .

But Ly's words were lost to Jenny in the pandemonium that occurred as the host of the ball appeared in a flash of fire atop a small, raised platform. It was the head of their Order, carrying the crown the Award winner would wear. Jenny swallowed hard. She knew she hadn't a chance, but every witch grew up wanting to win and Jenny was no exception.

"Ladies, Familiars, one and all—Welcome. I hope you have been enjoying the festivities so far. There is much more to come of course, but first, the nominations and the bestowing of the award."

Jenny tried to listen, but the nominations passed in a blur. Carnella and her cat, of course, and four other witches and their "normal" Familiars: A peacock, a fox, a mouse, and a frog. Jenny admitted they did some interesting magics, including the young nominee who was able to change her dress to match the peacock' s coloring. The winning criteria, of course, was how well the pairing was able to work together as well as how powerful the incantations were. Carnella was last and as Jenny expected, her display of fireworks emanating from the cat's tail was the most impressive of the five nominees.

Jenny. The cat. It's not her Familiar.

Jenny jerked to full attention. *What?*

It's Carnella doing all the work. The animal is just a cat.

Jenny squinted at Carnella. A slight sheen of sweat was marring Carnella's makeup. Jenny shook her head in disbelief. Ly was right. Carnella was straining to do the magic.

Jenny, back up. Something's about to happen. Something bad.

Jenny rose hastily and headed towards the back wall, and just in time. A mighty scream ripped the air, and Jenny looked up to see the ugliest vulture she had ever seen flap noisily around the room. Instantly the crowd parted, and Jenny saw that the creature was doing more than flying. Shouts of disgust and a strong pungent odor indicated the bird was actively showing its displeasure.

It flew towards Carnella and landed on her head. The cat, hissing and yowling, ran out the front door. The bird leaned over Carnella in a very vulture-like way, looking as though it was mad enough to peck out her eyes. Jenny wanted to laugh, but Carnella looked so mortified she only felt sorry for her.

"SILENCE!"

The room quieted instantly. It was a party, but everyone knew what their leader could do if provoked. The angry woman put her hands on her hips and stared at Carnella.

"Young lady, what exactly is going on?"

The vulture squawked loudly and a ripple of laughter crossed the room, stopping instantly as the crowd received a hard stare from the powerful witch.

Jenny watched in amazement as tears flowed down Carnella's face. Carnella looked at her feet, back up at the leader and tried to shake the bird from her head. The creature protested loudly, and a noxious odor once again caused many to cover their noses. Carnella started to flail wildly about; her actions were so comical the room once again erupted in laughter.

And then the energy shifted. If the Familiar had been irritated by Carnella's denial, it was furious at the crowd's seeming disrespect. Carnella screamed as the great bird raked its talons down the side of her face as it leaped from her head. The vulture filled the air with terrible, grating shrieks, circling as though deciding who would make the best prey. Jenny stared in horror as angry red eyes locked on hers. She was terrified, but knew she had to do something.

Ly, we have to help!

Yes. But what will we do? We haven't practiced—

I know, I know, but think . . . what are your natural talents? What do you do best as a slug?

Ly was silent for a moment. *Slime?*

Instantly a picture appeared in Jenny's mind; an early evening garden walk and the sparkling, delicate lines of slug tracks laced across the stone pathway. Jenny remembered the scrubbing it had taken to remove the stubborn strands. She had an idea of what to do, but would it work?

Ly! A weaving! Could we make some kind of cloth?

I think so. Take me out and hold me in front of you.

Jenny gently put her hand to her chest, and the slug slithered out of the shell. Jenny was surprised. It didn't feel slimy at all. It was rather silky, she thought distractedly.

She held out her hand as the vulture swooped towards her. Jenny turned her shoulder just in time to save Ly, but not herself. The vulture carved a long furrow down the side of one arm.

Jenny!

I'm all right. It's making another circle. We have time.

Jenny held out her hand again, blood dripping wetly from her wound. At first she tried mentally knitting something but found she was too nervous. *Perhaps something already in existence*, she thought, almost panic stricken now. *Maybe something at home.*

Jenny took a deep breath and tried again. In her mind she recreated the intricately patterned blanket on her bed. She imagined weaving a replica of the design; it appeared as a silvery after-image against her eyelids. Instantly she felt Ly's feathery touch, and the image disappeared.

Look, Jenny!

Jenny opened her eyes. Spread high overhead was a glittering blanket, looking exactly like the one at home. Unfortunately, directly underneath their creation was the vulture, preparing for another strike.

Jenny closed her eyes again in concentration. *Smother. Bind.*

She heard the crowd gasp and then a loud thump. When she opened her eyes this time the bird was trussed securely within the silvery cloth and lying on the floor in front of her. Surprisingly it didn't struggle, seemingly accepting its fate. As the nomination committee carried the vulture away it looked back at Jenny and Ly with sad, hollow eyes.

Jenny held the slug directly in front of her face. *You did that?*

We *did that.*

Jenny felt her arm being attended to and heard a thunderous applause as the Crown was placed on her head.

But her attention was only for her Familiar.

You really are quite wonderful. What else can

you—we—do?

She heard what she thought might be amusement and basked in a warmth unlike anything she had ever known.

Who knows? Jenny felt the twin eyestalks gently brush her hand. *We have the rest of our lives to find out.*

The Starship Expendable

E.J. Angel

Space. *The final frontier. These are the voyages of the Starship Expendable. Its five-hundred-fourteen year mission: To find new worlds, explore uncharted space . . . and to make a crap load of maps for the Intergalactic Map & Chart Co., Ltd., LLC, (c), TM, Patent Pending.*

Bren Torros took off her ear and stuck a microspanner in her head. Using the reflective surface of the egg-shaped portal window, she cycled her irises from brown, to gray, to green.

"Hot date, Torros?" A gray-clad crewman brushed past her in the narrow corridor, not breaking his stride as he gave her a smirk.

"Biosuite duty, smart ass," Bren shot back. "Green is my pollen guard."

"Nature finds a way, Torros!"

Bren flipped her retreating friend an interstellar bird and snapped her ear back on. Kahaar really could be an ass but he was also probably the only gray crew on board who didn't resent her. Plus he played a mean hand of *Go Fish*.

Bren straightened her own white uniform—albeit with its black command stripes—and started back down the outer ring.

There were two-hundred-eleven oval windows that circled the Expendable's outer corridor. Custom had it that when leaving dock, the ship's full compliment would gather one to each window and gaze out one last time.

Bren snorted. Her archival implant flashed Space Fleet vids of black uniformed crewmen standing at attention behind oval windows, watching their precious home planet shrink into the distance of space. "Sentimental schmucks."

Bren could care less about Chunkoid X4279. It had never been home. It had always been just the rock in space she was born on, 73rd rock from the Sun. The Expendable though. This ship was home.

She turned left, following the dimly luminescent green stripe in the floor, and hopped up on the green lift pad. The green tinted capsule closed around her and the lift began to move.

Usually Bren was focused on her job and her job

alone. As second in command, it was her duty to keep the crew working smoothly while the Captain planned their course. Bren had been on the Expendable for fourteen years and been Second for only one of those. In that year, there hadn't been a departmental mutiny, major mechanical misfortune or otherwise unpleasant brouhaha. But with a population of 73% gray crew to 36% white crew, it was an uphill battle . . . and one she loved.

When Bren was a teenager, with hardly a dozen cybernetics, she had obsessively dreamed of working her way up the ranks from a white-clad Commercially Commissioned Civilian Under Contract (CCCUC) to a gray suited Permanently Employed Navigational Intergalactic Spacefarer (she always forgot the acronym), all the way to a true officer in Space Fleet, donned in the ever-dashing (and always slimming) black.

But today, her career potential was an afterthought. She wasn't so interested in getting *into* her own black uniform as she was interested in getting Captain Martín Von Saint *out* of hers.

Lush, wet rainforest rose a hundred eighty feet into otherwise dead space. Protected by the organetics dome growing between the mechanical, arched framework, hundred year old cedars, red ferns as big as hovercrafts and seventy types—spongy, string, soggy, slimy, etc.—of moss, grew, sheltered lifeforms, ate carbon dioxide, belched oxygen and otherwise enabled the Expendable to exist. Every part of the ship, from the life support to the port duhcells to the warped cores was powered by some by-product of this hardy, musky, earthy, squishy ecosystem. And every part of Bren Torros was powered by the succulent sight of the sweat-slicked Martín Von Saint, her bare brown arm buried to the beautifully sculpted shoulder in a pond of primordial ooze.

"Captain," Bren's voice was weak.

Von Saint cast her a cursory glance, continuing to try to reach the underwater controls. "Specimen 742.8 died in ventricle intake tube thirty-three. I put it in the regeneration chamber but the blockage dropped the water temperature two degrees and the ameba reproductive cycles are discalculate by eight billion cells."

Good morning to you, too, Captain. "I thought something seemed off," Bren grinned and walked to a wall panel set into the dome's framework.

Squatting on the mossy earth, her black Space Fleet command uniform jacket discarded, leaving her in a black regulation labor top and black fatigues, Von Saint frowned up at Bren. "Was that humor, Number Two?"

Bren grimaced. She hated that title purely for juvenile reasons. Bren cast her a grin nonetheless.

"Yes, Captain, that was humor."

Von Saint snorted and tipped precariously forward in her attempt to locate the direct controls in the murky water. "I already tried the wall controls, Number Two. They weren't succinct enough."

Bren extended a hand and willed an organic fiber optic connection between her thumb and forefinger and the panel's incremental gauge. With her other hand she double-timed the access code strings into the alphanumeric touch pad, tapping the H_2O system for command priority alteration. "Just another few seconds, Captain. There. I've—"

SPLASH!

You're kidding me. Without pausing to properly disconnect, Bren tore away from the panel (that stung!) and vaulted over a nursery log. She kicked past a copse of standing nettles and displaced a quarter or ten trillion amoebas as she crashed into the pond and immediately sank . . . to her crotch.

Captain Von Saint, silky black hair unmussed from her sideways tumble but soaked by Bren's "rescue," wasn't smiling. "You're on my foot."

Inches away from Von Saint's bottomless nutmeg eyes, Bren felt pinned. "Sorry, Captain," Bren croaked but didn't move. She could smell the Captain's faint cherry blossom perfume . . . or was that algae? Bren's gaze dropped to the Captain's full mouth.

Von Saint abruptly brought her hand up in front

of her face. She checked the envirostat on her wrist. "Hm." The water temperature had stabilized. "Good work, Number Two." She turned and effortlessly lifted herself out of the pond.

Bren stared at her butt.

High above them, a stripe-tailed chipmunk mocked her.

"Let's get the other samples then, and—"

"Captain?"

Von Saint turned toward her as Bren followed suit and heaved herself out of the murk.

"Number Two?"

Bren took a deep breath. "Captain, may I speak freely?"

Von Saint just stared at her for what seemed like hours. Her intense gaze scrutinized Bren soundlessly, mercilessly. Just when Bren was about to withdraw her request (and crawl into a hole and die), the Captain solemnly nodded her head, "Continue."

"Martín, I—" Bren lost her nerve. She changed tactics. "Would you—"

Von Saint held up her hand and cut her off with a confident smile. "I know what you need to say, Number Two."

Bren blinked.

Von Saint put a hand on her shoulder. "Everyone onboard is talking about it."

Bren's jaw dropped. "They are?"

A not unfriendly chuckle. "Indeed. But that is how it is on a starship. It is a very insular existence. Dedication. Obsession. Passion. These things are bound to be noticed, even in spite of any inherit classism or personal jealousies."

Bren's brow creased. "What are you talking about, Martín?"

Von Saint smiled wider and squeezed Bren's shoulder. "As the only Space Fleet officer upon the Expendable, I chose to promote you above any gray crewmen because, quite simply, you are better. Yes, you're only CCCUC, but you surpass them all in skills and drive—"

"Martín—"

"You deserve those black stripes, Number Two. You are the best choice for second in command and the gray crew are simply going to have to get used to it. And—"

"Captain—"

"And, yes, Number Two, some day, when I know you're ready, I will sponsor your acceptance into Space Fleet and you will exchange your civilian whites for most honorable blacks. Perhaps you'll even want your own ship by then!" Von Saint slapped Bren's shoulder companionably. "Come now, Number Two. Don't concern yourself with the petty talk of lesser crewmen. Go close up that wall panel and we will finish our duties here."

With that, Von Saint trumped off into the forest, whistling tunelessly and taking readings with her envirostat.

Bren walked through the nettles (they stung), climbed over the nursery log, and plucked a handful of yellow and brown banana slugs off the wall panel. She stared at the blinking lights and moving gauges and tried to ignore the suddenly irritating beeps, blips and the chittering of the chipmunk. It didn't work. She clenched her fists. Her face burned red.

A moment later, Bren was staring into a twelve inch hole in the metal, hollow framework of the biosuite. Cybernetics or not, her fist would be sore and the control panel was destroyed.

A banana slug stretched one eye stalk toward the sparking hole. Bren flicked it away but the creature's sticky body just rolled down the wall a little ways and stuck there.

This was *not* Bren Torros' day.

Bren walked onto the bridge of the Expendable. She had taken the time to change out of her scummy uniform but her glower was still steely.

"Brr. It's cold in here. There must be a Torros in the atmosphere."

"Plug it, Kahaar."

Standing at his blue navigation station, Kahaar grinned.

Bren jabbed a finger toward a gray crewman and a

white crewman sitting at a red engineering dock. "Tomcatt. Zetta. Control panel seven in the biosuite needs replacing."

"Repair, Sir?" Zetta asked as she stood reluctantly.

Bren shot her a withering glare. "Did I say 'repair?'"

Tomcatt nodded curtly. "We'll replace it, sir." He gave Zetta a pointed look and the two exited the bridge.

Bren squinted her eyes after their departing figures then sank into her seat and pulled her viewbar across her lap. "Report."

Kahaar, as the next ranking crewman, provided the day's events. "Probe navigation of sectors Y-97 and Y-98 is complete and probes have been programmed to navigate sector Y-99 and Z-01 through Z-99.

"Navigation team on shift for downloading is Allan, DiMassa, Jasmine-Poel and Biel. They plan to have Y-97's data compiled by fourteen hundred hours.

"Engineering is ready for launch of the last Y-bound and all the Z-bound probes on your command."

Bren confirmed everything Kahaar was saying by deciphering the flashing lights and streaming binary code dashing across her viewbar. The icon assigned to probe Y-98 was flashing a bubonic purple with green spots. "Y-98 came back Command View Only?"

Kahaar shook his head. "No, Space Fleet View Only."

Bren glared at him but Kahaar met her eyes

seriously. He wasn't joking. She quickly looked at the other six gray crew on the bridge. A few looked back at her with frowns. No one was happy with 'Space Fleet View Only' results. If there was a classified anomaly any where in their A-Z cluster of sectors—in a Y sector no less—all their hard work mapping might be for naught.

In accordance with the law, Intergalactic Map & Chart Co., Ltd., LLC, (c), TM, Patent Pending, was assigned one Space Fleet captain per ship but IM&CC didn't make maps for the military. If Y-98 proved classified, the whole cluster would be shut to civilian travel and that meant no cluster map was needed. Which meant no map completion bonus.

"We're hoping it isn't another white hole, sir," admitted Sorensen from her navigation and launch station.

Bren frowned. The crew was still bent about that one. A little radiation spilling out of the business end of a black hole and the Captain had made sure the whole cluster was locked down for the "safety of the people." Bren had had her eyes on a smooth brown prax jacket with red neon piping, but no bonus had made that impossible.

Bren stood up. "Where is Herself, Kahaar?"

Kahaar grinned. "In her (Really) Ready Room, Sir."

Bren guffawed, "I wish."

The bridge's open com chimed and Tomcatt's voice filled the room. "Torros, Sir? Sir, we have a problem."

Now what? "Report."

Tomcatt's voice was panicked, "Sir, the biosuite alarms are going crazy. It seems—"

Zetta broke in, "Six specimens from the 914 set aren't reading as present in the biosuite and—"

"What?!" Bren found herself on her feet. Tomcatt and Zetta were talking over each other now, something about no force field over the hole in the control panel or a short circuit or something. Bren tapped into the life form database by squinting and looking down and to the left. What set was 914? Grizzly? Wolf? ...Slug?! Her voice sliced through the crewmen's chatter. "You're having a flipping fit over a half dozen obese worms? Are you serious?!"

"Sir!" Zetta admonished. "Every single life form in the biosuite is essential to the vital balance of the entire ecosystem and so the existence of life on the Expendable and—"

"Take my flipping dessert rations for the next six months and generate six new slugs, woman! Good Newton and Galileo! I've got *command* issues down here, people!" Bren was breathing heavily.

There was silence. Then Tomcatt's much more sedate voice, "Will do, sir. We're on it."

The comm chimed closed. "And next time," Bren

grumbled. "Don't call it in."

Bren clapped her hands together and pointed around the room. "All right. Let's multitask. Sorensen, Tam, WingWin, I want those hundred Z probes launched now. Lylan, Emond, get me Space Fleet's complete file on classified anomalies, decrypt it with command code SamTop.183xNoodle and route it to my viewbar. Swinsinski, hustle it down to the nav download team and light a plasma flare under their butts. I—"

There was a chorus of *yes, sirs* and Bren grinned. *Damn if I won't win over these gray crew.* She straightened her uniform and lifted her chin. "I am going in there." And she strode toward the black door of the Captain's Ready Room.

"Go get her, tiger."

Bren flipped him a second (timeless) bird. "You have the bridge, Kahaar."

Then things happened all at once:

Bren raised her hand to tap the door chime.

"Probes Y-99 and Z-01 through z-30, launched!" Sorensen announced.

The Ready Room opened with a swish. "Don't—" Captain Von Saint called out.

"Probes Z-31 through Z-65, launched!" Tam added.

"—launch—" Von Saint rushed through the Ready Room's door.

"Probes Z-66 through Z-99, launched!" WingWin punched the big blue button.

"—the probes!" And Von Saint collided with Bren full force, both women, a tangle of limbs like a zebra in a blender, toppling like a mass of cause and effect dominos, emperor penguins down an icy slope, salt and pepper spilling out of space age double-grav shakers, or any other number of white and black things with the sole exception of nuns tripping on their habits on a foggy morning in May in the Himalayan hills.

"Captain?!" Several voices asked in unison.

Von Saint, Bren pinned full length beneath her, pushed herself half way up, hands braced against the floor on either side of Bren's head. "There's a malfunction. Probe Y-98 scanned in as classified but there was no anomaly. There's something wrong—"

A klaxon blared. An umber light flashed.

Kahaar jabbed frantically at his engineering controls. "We've got five—no six!—probes lodged at various points in their jettison tubes. Eject and flush commands have no effect." Kahaar looked up from his screen, his normally handsome brown face ashen. "The probes are overheating, Captain."

"If's fa flugs!"

Von Saint looked down at Bren. "What was that, Number Two?"

Ignoring her surely imminent stroke, Bren

casually turned her face away from the Captain's C-cups. "It's the slugs, Captain. They've jammed the probes."

In less than two minutes, Bren and Von Saint had transported to the jettison deck and stepped into their snap-on spacesuits. Both suits, from helmets to oxygen tanks, boots to body gloves, were bright green.

Bren opened an emergency locker and removed a massive probe vac. Vacs were usually manned by mechonoids but the Expendable didn't have any androids. It only had Bren. She dialed up her muscle mass and cocked the vac back. She grinned at Von Saint through her helmet. "Lock and load, Captain."

Von Saint nodded and touched her suit-to-bridge comm patch. "We're going out, Kahaar."

Kahaar's voice answered in their helmets. "I can give you two, maybe three second warning before a probe blows, Sirs. That's it."

Von Saint nodded again. "Understood." She turned to Bren and spoke on their suit-to-suit channel. "Ready, Number Two?"

Bren felt adrenaline surge through her body. "Always, Captain."

Von Saint smiled and opened an access hatch in the floor.

The Expendable was a study in absurdist neo geo. Imagine an egg, lying on its side, with a white and black tire looped around the middle length studded with reflective oval windows, a green dome rising from the top of the egg, a red tomato stuck on the back nestled between two silver, red-striped dorsal fins, and a blue sea urchin, spikes and all, stuck upside down to the egg's belly.

It was among these hundred spines—the blue, cylindrical probe jettison tubes—that Bren and Von Saint now walked. Their ultramag boots sent vibrations up their legs with each step but the boots also safely adhered the two women, upside down, to the blue metallic surface beneath the Expendable and stopped them from floating off into the endless universe, which would most certainly suck.

Captain Von Saint waved a duhranium locator along a six foot blue jettison tube marked with a white number 32. "We have a probe lodged at two feet from the mouth, Number Two. Prepared to siphon?"

Bren gave a jaunty thumbs up affirmative and, with the ultramag soles of her boots turned to adhere to the tube thirty-two, began to shimmy up the tube. *You better be looking at my butt while I'm risking my life here.* She couldn't help the thought.

Bren couldn't make herself peer down the barrel of the tube—how stupid would that be?—so she just slung the vac hose off her shoulder and slapped it hard over the tube's mouth. "Ignition!" she called, then a sudden roar from the vac, a rumble from the tube, then—POP!—and Bren cut the power, ripped the vac off the tube and—WHOSH!—the duhranium probe dashed on its was as if it had never threatened to blow holes in the belly of the ship.

Bren reached down into the tube. Alas, she came out empty handed; Only a thin layer of slime remained of the wayward little traveler. "To stardust then, sticky fellow," she murmured, and shimmied down number thirty-two.

They worked quickly as they could, moving among the metal forest of blue spires and Bren actually managed—remarkably!—to recover, alive, three of the six missing slugs from their tubular misadventures. She sealed them in biomatter stasis pockets built into her suit and then freed their temperamental, easily discouraged duhranium counterparts.

"The nav probes should be as resilient as these worms," Bren commented as she reattached her boots to the ground after freeing the fifth probe. She smiled at the rescued banana slug, sleeping it all off in the transparent stasis pocket on her arm.

Von Saint wasn't listening. Bren could tell from the beads of sweat on the Captain's brow that she was getting worried. "Tube 29. This one. Probe is thirteen inches from the mouth."

"That close?" Bren tried to ignore her own

pounding heart, joking, "I should just be able to kick the tube and knock the probe out!"

Von Saint didn't smile but Bren was already climbing. Toward the end of the tube, Bren stopped short. She hit her suit-to-bridge patch. "Hey, Kahaar? You're not asleep are you?"

Her friend's voice sounded strained but calm. "No. Are you? You should be done by now."

"Space walk is a delicate thing, Kahaar. How come tube 29 is shaking?"

A moment then, "The probe is revving, trying to continue launch. It's stable though. You can continue extraction."

Bren put a gloved hand flat against the tube. The metal was trembling something awful.

"Number Two, don't risk it." The Captain's voice, just suit-to-suit, was near a breaking point. "Let engineering try another eject."

Kahaar's voice was loud in Bren's helmet. "I'm seeing some heat fluctuations, sirs. It's now or never."

Bren set her jaw. She pushed up the last few feet of the tube and slapped the vac over the mouth. "Ignition," she called but the sound was lost under Kahaar's shout.

"Torros! Get off! It's going to—"

"Bren!"

The probe was two feet in diameter, solid duhranium, and it made a deafening boom as it exploded in a shower of shrapnel, blasting from the jettison tube with enough force to break the vac's seal and shred the hose. Bren was whipped away from the tube, straight out into space, until something—perhaps her wildly flailing arms and legs—swung her momentum around and her ultramags tugged her toward an undamaged tube. Sweet magnetism.

Kahaar was still shouting and someone else, too. And there was a bizarre hissing noise. Bren tagged a tube with one foot, reassured by the solid hold, and pulled herself in.

All at once, Von Saint was halfway up the tube, pulling Bren down, wrapping her arms around her, calling her by her first name. "Bren, hurry! Come on! By Galileo, Bren, hurry!" Von Saint's face was clearly panicked.

Bren tried to frown in confusion but could only smile. Their boots connected with the blue floor at the same time. "I'm okay, Captain. Really."

Von Saint met her gaze with an openly terrified expression. "Bren, your air tank was punctured."

The hissing sound. Bren looked into the Captain's eyes. They were moist. They both glanced toward the entrance hatch. There were seventy or more jettison tubes to maneuver around between here and there. The hiss from the air tank was already slowing; There wasn't much more oxygen to vent.

"We can share tanks!" Von Saint suddenly said,

and she reached back, not thinking. Bren grabbed her hand.

"Captain, these suits don't work that way. You'll just vent your air. We'll both be at risk."

"Bren. . . . " Von Saint shook her head.

Bren managed a grin. "What are we waiting for, Martín? The sooner we get going the less distance you'll have to carry me."

Von Saint set her jaw. She grabbed Bren's gloved hand tightly and led her away at a good clip.

A little more than twenty minutes later, Bren ripped off her helmet and collapsed against the wall of the jettison dock gasping. She was drenched in sweat, her heart pounding. Leaning beside her, helmet discarded, gazing at Bren fiercely and with wonderment, Captain Martín Von Saint was transfixed.

"That," Von Saint whispered. "Was incredible."

Bren rolled her head to the side slowly and smiled.

Von Saint kissed her. Then, "Tonight. My quarters. Dinner. Then sex." And the Captain touched Bren's face, her eyes smoldering, and walked from the room.

Kahaar stepped up and helped Bren strip off her damaged suit. He grinned wickedly. "Are you going to tell her during dinner that cybernauts can go an hour without oxygen?"

Bren grinned back at him. "No. Not dinner. I'll tell

her during sex. . . . Or not."

Kahaar's laughter echoed in the big room as Bren walked steadily out into the corridor, following the green stripe in the floor back to the biosuite to return her three slimy little charges to their ecosystem.

Escargot

Marshall Miller

s that what I think it is?" Robert "Bob" Renfro said as he pointed at the oversized video screen.

"Well, what do you think it is?" replied his totally ginger wife, Chauncey.

"It looks like a snail, Chauncey."

"Actually, my dear husband, it is a slug. It looks like a hugely overgrown banana slug, similar to what I used to spread salt on in the Pacific Northwest."

"Salt? Why?"

"Why, to kill them. See what you missed growing up in Arizona?"

Bob ran his hands through his dark red hair. All his friends told him that redheads marrying were a recipe for disaster due to the well-known ginger temper. However, to Bob, the ginger love and passion made up for any anger issues.

"Yeah," he answered. "And people used to make fun of me when I talked about dumping scorpions into ant nests to watch them fight."

"We killed slugs because they ate our gardens," explained Chauncey, "not for shits and giggles."

"Oh, come on, Saucy. You liked watching them die. By the way, how did the salt kill them?"

Saucy was a pet name Bob had bestowed on his wife when they were boyfriend/girlfriend. Some women may have been offended by its undertones, but not Chauncey. Actually, she regaled about how she was a hot-looking ginger, auburn hair, sexy body and all. Chauncey was a liberated female exobiologist who knew how to use her sex appeal to get what she wanted, especially with her husband.

"Well, mister astrophysicist martial artist, it dries out their mucus covering. Slugs and snails are the originators of the concept of slime trails. They travel on a large 'foot' which secretes a mucus that protects the foot membrane as it uses muscular contraction to move at the proverbial snail's pace."

"Slime trail, huh."

A mischievous look in Bob's eyes must have tipped off Chauncy that his mind was going someplace it shouldn't as there was a flash in her eyes as she warned, "If you are thinking about a certain rude and crude joke men make about women being bipedal, I will thump you so hard..."

"Hey, the Alien Slug is moving." Bobs observation snapped the two scientists back from their musings to the serious subject at hand.

For the overgrown slug was a member of the Arrivals, an alien species which had been traveling decades to reach Earth. Just over twenty-five years before, the first messages began reaching the then-called Earth II created planetoid. A masterpiece of the asteroid belt "Rock Hounds" who joined six large asteroids into a mini-moon, it took the personnel there, and Space Command personnel from Earth, to discover the Arrivals were trying to warn humans of some past conflict which still posed a danger. Unfortunately, the warning came too late. A UXB, an Unexploded Bomb from some ancient war, destroyed Earth II before the message was deciphered. Fragments crashed to Earth and the Moon, killing thousands in addition to the three thousand inhabitants of Earth II.

That was when Space Command took over. The privatization of Outer Space nascent in the early twenty-first century came to a screeching halt in 2101. Thus, Bob and Chauncey were on the Space Command Vessel ARTHUR C. CLARKE, the only anti-matter drive spacecraft in existence. Fifteen days of acceleration out, fifteen in braking and the ship with fifty-two souls on board was out at the dwarf planet Pluto.

The broadcast video came from a hollowed out piece of rock, one of six the aliens used as Starcraft.

Some two thousand clicks away, it appeared to have a similar form of space drive based on the energy signatures, though possibly more advanced. The odd fact was the six 'space rocks' were almost the same mass as the six used to create the late Erath II. Assumptions were made the craft must contain a similar available interior space.

"How big is our... friend?" asked Bob.

"Based on the earlier information and videos I have reviewed, about the same size as a Kodiak bear." Chauncy adjusted the contrast controls for the video.

"And it does seem to be a yellow hue. So, a giant banana slug is a good description."

As the exobiologist spoke, the Arrival creature displayed two characteristics besides its size that set it apart from the Earthbound versions. A pair of long tentacles deployed from the creature's back mantle. The specialized appendages had six digits on the end of each tentacle arranged in a star shape. These "fingers" had already displayed excellent abilities, just like the human hand, to interact and mold the environment of the Arrivals. In layman terms, they created and used tools.

"Time for another writing lesson," said Chauncy. Her husband helped her send the necessary commands and signals required to arrange the cameras and other recording devices in the Box as Chauncy 'talked' with the Arrival via a computer screen. The confidence and apparent nonviolent nature of the arriving aliens had been demonstrated early on by their ready agreement to enter the Box, a massive airlock equipped structure the humans had created as a meeting room of the two species. Decontamination systems enabled space suited humans to rendezvous with the aliens in the Box. However, only when the Arrivals asked to meet. After some twenty-five years of study, the alien language indicated *they* wanted to be the instigator of face to face meetings. Bob looked at his wife.

"You sure you're ready for this face to face?"

"What kind of exobiologist would I be if I was afraid to meet the first alien sentient species which contacted humanity? Plus, we have communicated with them for a quarter century, based on warnings of an ancient danger."

Bob frowned as he replied, "Well, as long as they eat plants like your home grown slugs."

"Actually, by dear, there are predatory slugs that even eat their own kind, They have lots of teeth." Chauncy gave her husband the best shit-eating grin she could produce as his mouth dropped open.

The Box deployed out from the ARTHUR C. CLARKE using attached remote-controlled rocket thrusters. A long and durable cable kept it attached to the Earthship. Two kilometers out, the Box was at the end of its tether. Inside the Box awaiting the aliens to arrive was Chancy and the Space Command medical officer, a Doctor Azubuike Baba. His size and strength had made Bob feel more secure when Commander of the CLARKE, General Samara Kravitz, had refused to allow Bob to accompany his wife on this first face to face meeting.

"Can't risk allowing your natural proclivity to protect your wife get in the way of some possibly odd communications," said the small and lithe raven-haired senior officer.

Samara had been a orbital fighter pilot, then an early space patrol craft commander. The general exuded a presence and strength out of proportion with her just over five-foot frame. Then again, in Space, smaller and lighter meant more efficient use of available space and supplies.

"Oh come on, General," Bob had tried to argue. "I may be a civilian now, but I'm a combat Vet. I know how to control myself."

"You weren't in combat with your spouse, Doctor Renfroe. I bet you that you would have reacted differently had Chauncy been along."

"You bet he would," his wife had interjected. "Bob would try and sicc me on the enemy. He knows I'm meaner than he is."

General Kravitz had ignored the attempt at humor.

"My decision has been made, Robert. You can stay in the control room and monitor all the energy emissions from the Arrival craft. We need some signal intelligence about just how more advanced they are than us."

Thus, here they were. Bob watching an array of screens and sensors as an egg-shaped alien shuttle craft approached the Box.

"You friends are closing to one hundred meters, Chauncy," Bob broadcast over a secure network. Although the need of a secure audio net was in question.

"Any written messages?" his wife asked.

"Not since they sent the one saying they were leaving their ship."

"Well, we're ready on this end," said his wife.

"You watch out for all those slug teeth you told me about, Chauncy," said Bob.

"No worries, my friend," Azubuike interjected. "I will ensure no one touches a red hair on your wife's head."

Bob laughed. He had grappled some with Az at the gym and knew just how powerful he was. But fighting something the size of a Kodiak Grizzly? That was another story.

"The crew of the CLARKE will not allow any harm to come to the only other civilian on this ship," Samara

Kravitz interjected. "So no worries." Bob kept forgetting this was a party line, not a private one.

"Yes, Ma'am," answered Bob.

"Any new intelligence on the shuttlecraft?" asked the General.

"It's emanating some magnetic signatures," replied the astrophysicist. "We're still experimenting with some magnetic drives, also examining their use in artificial gravity technology."

"So they are more advanced, But maybe by not much," opined the General.

"Okay, the shuttle is sliding up next to the Box. No signs of rockets so the Arrivals must be using magnetism to control their docking."

"No felt contact here," said Chauncy. She turned and smiled at Az through her helmet faceplate. The large man gave her a thumbs up sign and shifted his magnetized booted feet. History was about to be made in zero-G, whether for good or ill.

"Okay, hang on to your hat," broadcast Bob. "Our friends are sliming the airlock."

"What?" said his wife. "That is weird."

"For what purpose?" interjected the General.

"The shuttle may be organic, biological in nature," Bob stated. "Not my field of expertise, but if electric eels can generate voltage, maybe our friends can play with magnetic currents."

"The airlock is cycling," Az broadcast. Suddenly,

everyone seemed to hold their breath.

Chauncy stared at the airlock door. The green indicator light flashed, then became a steady gleam, signifying the inner door could be opened safely without danger of decompression.

"Az, think we need to open the door for them?" She asked

"Let's see if they can figure it out. That will tell us they have minds of their own."

Moments later, the airlock door unlatched and swung open. As it did, a massive translucent bubble pushed its way into the center of the meeting space. As the bubble expanded into the room, Chauncy and Az saw two of the aliens entered. The exobiologist observed the two slug creatures moved on the rhythmic muscular contractions of the single large foot, characteristic of terrestrial gastropods.

"That bubble must act like a protective suit," said Az.

"Yes," replied Chauncy. She was having trouble putting her thoughts into words as the uniqueness of the event slapped her in her mental face. My God, Aliens! But ones who looked like some of the simpler life forms on Earth. Finally, the scientist mentally shook herself into action.

"See those two long stalk tentacles on the top of its head, Az? Those are eyestalks. And it looks the eyes are as developed as ours."

"I seem to remember Earth gastropods eyes are more just light and motion receptors," said the medical doctor. "These look like they can give us a proper examination."

"Yes, Az. And the lower two are like noses. Earth forest slugs have a sensitive sense of smell."

"Any auditory organs, Chauncy?"

"On Earth, no. These have a bump between their nose stalks that we think senses vibrations but is not a true ear. The Arrivals use audio frequencies for very little."

"How do they... talk?"

"Watch, Az. You'll find out."

The giant bubble parted and retracted back to the airlock. As it did, the exobiologist saw the substance of the protective bubble looked like a form of mucus.

"Az, the bubble, It's from body excretions."

"I guess I was right about their use of organics," Bob interjected.

"Don't get swell-headed, dear," replied Chauncy.

The giant versions of a Pacific Northwest Banana Slug moved slowly closer. Chauncy watched the two sets of eye stalks shifting and moving and surmised the creatures were examining the humans as they were studying the Arrivals.

"Bob, what's the air quality? Is it safe to take our helmets off?"

"The sensors say yes, Chauncy."

"Az, we have exchanged images over time with our visitors, but without these suits. Feel comfortable removing your helmet?"

The large man smiled as he replied, "You're the expert on aliens. I'm just a lowly ships MD."

"You think this is wise, Doctor Renfroe?" It was the General reminding the scientists that the CLARKE's crew was listening in.

"It is necessary due to the information we have on how they communicate with each other, General."

There was momentary silence, then the General replied, "Okay. I have the Tactical Response Team standing by in the shuttle if things go south."

The two humans helped each other remove their helmets and tucked them under their arms. As Chauncy and Az removed their suit helmets, the Arrivals twisted their eye stalks at different angles. The humans headsets would still provide communication links.

"They are definitely giving us the once over," observed the exobiologists. Then the alien to their left pulled a meter square piece of a transparent substance from a hidden fold on the mantle. Holding it in one six-digit hand, it began to rub its fingers on the surface. In a minute, the Arrival had traced on the tablet a series of darkening lines. It then held it up for the human's perusal.

"Bingo," said Chauncy. "The writing spells out 'We

Greet.' Now it's my turn."

Chauncy unfolded a large screened computer tablet attached to her suit leg and turned it on. Quickly, she traced some symbols the aliens had broadcast over the years as they approached the Sol System. The scientist turned it so the aliens could read it.

"Their version of 'Hello, how are you,' General."

Upon reading the message, a strong smell of cinnamon assaulted the human's noses.

"First valid contact, my friends, with them using a personal interspecies language. Now if we can keep from sneezing, we figure out a way to tell them we get it."

"They communicate by odors and smell?" asked General Kravitz.

"We believed so. However, until we met face to face, experienced it, we could not be sure." Chauncy removed a small bulb from a velcro pocket on her thigh. When she squeezed the bulb, a little puff of powder floated in the air. It toke just moments for the aliens to react. They raised their heads up on their thick necks and opened their mouths.

"Watch it, Saucy," warned her husband.

The alien traced a new message on the transparent board. It held the board up so Chauncy could see it. She grinned when she read it.

"You Friend Smell. Vanilla is the scent of

friendship. We are cooking with gas, people!"

The ships crew and the scientists had a celebration after the initial two-hour visit. Chauncy was both tired and pumped as she sipped at her moonshine drink. Samara Kravitz had looked the other way when Bob Renfroe produced a gallon of good old Arizona Bust Head. The astrophysicist had a minor in chemistry.

"So, Ma'am," young Lieutenant Lucia Perez asked, "what do you think is the alien's purpose for traveling all this way to warn us?" Chauncy shrugged.

"We have been trying to communicate at arms length. Actually, *super* arms length as we have been communicating over lightyears for some twenty-five years. So, now that we are face to face, talking without years, or even hours delay, we can get down to the nitty-gritty."

"Did I tell you my brilliant wife here also has a Masters in Linguistics?" Bob interjected as he put his arm around Chauncy's waist. She kissed him on the cheek.

"And now, my husband. I am exhausted, and your moonshine is going straight to my head. Time to hit the sack."

"Your wish is my command, oh great slug queen."

Chauncy slapped his shoulder, then grabbed his hand and began to lead him out of the room. The artificial gravity created by the spin of the vast cylindrical ARTHUR C. CLARKE meant they did not have to waste time trying to walk with magnetic boots. As the left the meeting room, General Kravitz approached.

"You did an excellent job, Chauncy," Samara said. "Get some rest. When is the next scheduled meeting?"

"Forty-Eight hours from now, General. I have preparation to do. The Arrivals are still trying to grasp important cultural ideas from our language, seeing what makes us tick. Just like we are trying to do with their. Saying hello is one thing. Discussing how we view ourselves as a species... that is something else."

"My ship and personnel are at your disposal, both of you. I hope, Bob, you can glean some more information about their starfaring technology."

"Will do, Ma'am. Now, if you will excuse us, I think my wife needs some downtime."

Ten minutes later, the Renfroes were in their private quarters. The Space Command personnel lived primarily in crowded bunks and sleeping bays. Except for the ships commander, the General, who also had her private quarters also. As the married couple stripped and climbed into the small shower together, Chauncy hugged, then kissed her husband.

"Hmmm. So yellow banana slugs excite you. Or is it being near a certain dark Mandingo... *Ouch!* You bit me."

"I'll knee you in the family jewels if you keep that

crap up." Saucy Chauncy kissed him again, slow and sexy. Then she looked into her lovers eyes.

"I just have this... *feeling* that there is something I am missing."

"Like what?" asked Bob. "We have been communicating for a quarter of a century, based on them warning us about some danger or threat. This meeting near Pluto is to understand better what happened millennia ago."

"Well, for one thing, they are confused about our binary gender and sexual reproduction."

"How so, Saucy?" Bob nibbled her neck as they pressed their nude bodies together under the recycled water. No one thought about it being recycled urine. Chauncy giggled a bit, then nibbled her husband's ear.

"You mean they don't fool around in the shower like we do?" asked Bob.

"They are true hermaphrodites, just like Earth Slugs. A clear case of parallel evolution," answered Chauncy.

"Well, with their science, biology like the manipulation of mucus material to form protective bubbles, why can't they understand?"

"Many cultures have blind spots. Like when we humans thought homosexual desire was a perversion rather than a biological and genetic sexual variation in some."

"So, my sexy wife, they do the nasty and can both

be poked and poke, both get pregnant. Yes?"

"You hit it on the head. They lay eggs, we believe, rather than give birth. I have to pin that concept down with them. Which may be difficult since they communicate with their own kind using odors and excreted smells."

"But they have a written language."

Chauncy frowned. "As an adjunct to their communication by smells. Some insects, like ants, lay scent trails, seem to communicate basic concepts by smells. Hell, some mammals exude strong musk scents to tell others 'here I am, and horny' like moose, elephants."

"But most higher animals on Earth have a lot of sights and sounds in their communication," said Bob.

"That's it. That is the area of difficulty. I studied the works of Helen Keller. She was blind and deaf, but learned to communicate, even speak after a fashion."

They scrubbed each others backs as they both thought about the concept of a smell-based language. Then Chauncy spoke.

"Well, I won't solve the mysteries in the shower. I'm too tired."

"So, I guess that is a hint that anything rising to the occasion is a waste of time," said Bob. Chauncy smiled impishly.

"Did I tell you Earth slugs sometimes amputate the others version of a penis during mating?"

"Well, that sure gets this man in the mood. Pardon me while I see if the machinist on board can make me an armored jock strap."

Chauncy laughed then clutched her love. "Come here, fool, and love me."

The next meeting in the Box lasted four hours. When Chauncy and Az returned to the CLARKE, the exobiologist asked to meet with Bob and the General in private. Samara had them come to her private quarters. There, the ship and mission commander poured them each a glass of brandy.

"Medicinal purposes," Samara Kravitz said with a smile.

"Now, Chauncy. What is the concern?"

"They keep pressing me about this whole reproduction thing," the exobiologist said with a frown.

"How so?"

"They seem to assume that our genders mate with whomever, don't seem to have long term relationships. I tried to explain that I have a mate, Bob here, not Az. They also seem a little confused about our variations in pigmentation, as all adult Arrivals, Slugs, are banana yellow." Chauncy paused in thought.

"So what do they want, specifically?" asked the General.

"They want to meet my mate, and I believe watch

us have sex to prove how we interact."

"Oh, that's great," interjected Bob. "Voyeurist aliens. Probably record us for an interstellar broadcast."

"I think that is part of the problem," added Chauncy.

"How so?" asked Samara again.

"They have intercepted a crapload of our signals, broadcasts. Some of those must have been pornographic, based on their attempts at inquiries." Chauncy released an exasperated sigh. "They have seen lesbian and gay activities, and don't understand when I say most of humanity are heterosexual, that we have to have a male and a female to reproduce."

"What in holy Hell does that have to do with the 'warning from space' they kept broadcasting?" Bob asked.

"Nothing other than this seemed to derail their whole thought process. It's as if the Slugs need to understand us before they fully explain the historical threat. Why? I have no idea. We are dealing with an alien species of overgrown gastropods, who use smells to communicate."

General Kravitz poured some more brandy, then sat in thought. Finally, she took a sip and set her drink down.

"Are you two willing to, how we say, perform? If it meant humanity learning this threat, the Arrivals keep mentioning?"

The married scientists looked at each other.

"This is bizarre," said Chauncy.

"No leaked recordings. Right?" asked Bob.

"No video hookup if you do this. Just audio. For security. You two need to be able to yell for help if necessary."

"Man, I signed on for God and humanity," said Bob. "I did not think it would mean making a sex education tape for some slugs!"

The next meeting was scheduled for forty-eight hours after the last. Bob made sure all of his scientific findings based on signal intelligence were up to date. Electronic emissions from the Arrivals had provided him with a wealth of information on the status of their technology. They seemed to be a long-lived species, living on a planet with much less gravity than Earth, possibly as much as half. Which may explain how they could grow so large. They had been a starfaring species for at least a thousand years. However, despite all his and others analysis, the Threat or who left things like the UXB that destroyed Earth II was still nebulous.

He and Chauncy were suited up and ready to go in the Box. He smiled at his wife through his helmet visor. "So, Saucy, did you wear some sexy negligee to get me all excited?" he asked with his best leering gaze.

"And since when was that necessary, Mr.

Horndog? All I have ever had to do was wiggle my ass or bend over..."

"*Hey*! People are listening."

"Well, Bob, you brought it up."

"Are you two ready?" the General interjected.

"Ready as we'll ever be," replied the exobiologist. "Of course, with women, performance anxiety is not that big a deal. Just some lubrication..."

"You just have to get graphic," Bob shot back. Samara Kravitz could not repress a laugh. When she became a General in Space Command, she never thought she would be overseeing two humans demonstrating sexual relations to Aliens

"Well, to be serious for a moment," said the General. " I realize what you two are about to do is risky. We assume the Arrivals are advanced enough to adjust to different behavior they see for the first time. Not like Christian Missionaries screaming at seeing bare-breasted indigenous people."

"But," she continued, "we still have not really gotten inside their brains. So, we all suppose this is a clinical exchange of information. Just be advised I have a Tactical Response Team sitting in a shuttle if things go south."

"Like, as in the Slugs want to test their thousand plus teeth on human flesh," stated Bob.

"Exactly. Robert, Chauncy. God speed. We know this is a sacrifice of your privacy. It will not be forgotten."

"No photos, right?" Asked Bob.

"No photos."

The Box was reeled out on the two-kilometer tether, and the humans waited. Bob had looked at the ARTHUR C. CLARKE as the Box reached the end of its line. A large cylinder size of an Earth naval aircraft carrier set inside of a perfect cross of four anti-matter engines. Two were used to accelerate, two to decelerate, which prevented the need of turning the spaceship around. Bob was still trying to figure out how the Arrivals mounted their engines on their asteroid starships. All he knew was by their energy signatures; they were a form of anti-matter engines. The magnetic propulsion systems of their shuttles were still a mystery.

Eventually, the egg-shaped alien shuttle slid up next to the Box and again accessed the airlock using mucus pseudopods. As before, two creatures entered the meeting room in a sizeable mucus membrane structure.

"Same two?" ask Bob.

"Looks like them. I can now identify slight differences in the eye stalks."

One of the Arrivals displayed the writing tablet with the "We Greet" written on it. Chauncy wrote on her tablet a serious of symbols in their language.

"I just told them it is good to meet again, and that

we are ready with a demonstration to answer their questions."

"Did you ever ask them what they call themselves?" asked Bob. "I mean, we say we are humans or people."

"Well, let me ask them again. Maybe our Slug friends will share more now that we agreed to share more."

The Arrivals looked at what the exobiologist had written and quickly responded. Chauncy read it out loud.

"Good Folk. They see themselves as the Good Folk. Now, they want to see how binary genders reproduce." Chauncy set the tablet down and began to strip. A nervous Bob followed her example, as they secured their clothes to a small bench bolted to the floor.

"I hope this Box is warm enough," stated Bob. "If a certain something shrivels up, they may get the wrong idea."

"Well, I have a solution to that. Keep you magnetic shoes on, or you will float around."

"Yeah. Which begs the question of sex in zero-G. Every action results in a ... Hey!"

Saucy Chauncy began to gently caress a vital part of Bob's body if the demonstration was to be a success.

"Now, here you were, all worried and you are already rising to the occasion."

Bob looked into his wife's eyes, then leaned over and kissed her.

"Samara promised no video," he said as their mouths parted.

"Why, you changed your mind? You want a selfie?"

"Just maybe something to watch in old age, my love. Now, how do we... do it without floating around."

"Here, attach these magnetic strips to the floor. Then face me."

In a few moments, Chauncy floated up to the extent of the straps, then maneuvered herself down, sliding slowly along Bobs body. With his feet still in the magnetic shoes, Chauncy mounted him, the couple using free hands to make sure part A went into slot B.

"That feels... nice," said the astrophysicist.

"Just nice? How about if I use my Kegels?"

"God. When did I last tell you how much I love you, Saucy?"

"Before we came over here, Lover. Now kiss me. You fool."

The two humans became as one, with Chauncy's arms and legs wrapped around her husband. Zero-G meant zero weight on your partner, so it became a matter of matching thrusting and response actions.

Later, the question would be did Zero-G Sex result in a head-busting mutual orgasms or was it due to the partners desire to further the successful contact with the aliens now known as Good Folk?

The two loves untangled themselves, and then Chauncy maneuvered towards her secured suit.

"Now to use some hand wipes to take care of a certain genetic material..."

Chauncy never finished the action nor the comment.

At unprecedented speed, a mucus pseudopod moved and engulfed the two Homo sapiens. Bob tried to kick and hit it as Chauncy screamed and fought. It was if they were fighting foam rubber. The humans and the two Good Folk encased in the organic material were sucked back into the alien shuttlecraft as it left the Box.

General Samara Kravitz screamed in rage.

In minutes the naked humans were dumped on the floor of the shuttlecraft room. Bob helped his wife to her feet.

"A slight artificial gravity is in here. We are not floating around."

"Why did you do this, you sonsabitches," Chauncy yelled.

"If they have no real ears, screaming at them is a waste of time."

Three Good Folk slugs moved into the room.

"New ones?" Asked Bob.

"I think so. These slugs have communication

tablets. And smell all that vanilla and cinnamon? They are trying to tell us we are friends and calm us down."

One of the Good Folk extended the tablet towards Chauncy with its long tentacle. She took it and read the message, then snorted derisively.

"Friend? Good Folk? Really?" The exobiologist angrily wrote a reply on the tablet.

"I just tried to say friends don't slime friends without permission."

"Think it will work?"

"Hell, I don't know. What I do know is I don't believe these slugs understand the concept of very angry apes coming for their comrades."

The three overgrown banana slugs began to fill the air with unusual combinations of odors and scents.

"They are talking with each other, maybe arguing," said Chauncy.

"It's beginning to smell like a fart contest. Whew!" Her husband said as he held his nose. One of the slugs shoved a tablet towards Chauncy. She took it and read it aloud with a frown.

"What do you mean, you need to know who we are? We have communicated with you for a quarter century, meet with you, and you say you don't know who we are? You called us, Fuckers!" Chauncy began to write an angry reply.

Something slammed into the shuttle, and in the light gravity, all the beings were sent flying. Organic padding on the floor and walls kept the humans from being injured other than a possible bruise or two. The artificial gravity held, and Bob stood up.

"I could do a John Carter on Barsoom, jump around and slash them with this tablet," he said to his wife.

"And wind up feeling what a thousand plus teeth feel like. Wait, Bob. We'll get a chance to show you don't screw with Gingers."

The illumination and lighting went out.

"Aw, fuck," said Bob in the darkness.

Then human Hell came to the slugs.

Lt. Lucia Perez led the Space Marines into the breached section of the alien shuttle craft moments after their craft rammed the slugs. The humans had all trained for a high G acceleration assault, so none were stunned into inactivity in their combat suits. Their electromagnetic bolt guns fired the equivalent of three-inch long steel nails at hypervelocities. The projectiles struck at such high speed they send shock waves through whatever they hit. Within seconds, Good Folk slugs were being shredded. The room the Renfroes were in had sealed automatically when the alien's craft hull was breached. Through trial and error, the dozen assault troops found the correct place of confinement in some ten minutes. They had brought two space rescue pods with them, used controlled explosives to breach the walls, and encapsulated the two scientists before catastrophic decompression could harm them.

A second human shuttle picked up all the personnel, there being no fatalities.

The first assault shuttle, impaling the alien craft, hurtled towards the nearest asteroid starship. The second shuttle accelerated at two Gs using solid fuel propulsion thrusters. There was over a thousand klicks to travel in record time as the ARTHUR C. CLARKE prepared for battle.

Samara Kravitz met the Refroes with a medical team after the shuttle docked in the bay. The General tried to force the two scientists to rest in sickbay, but they refused.

"We have to communicate with them," said Chancy. "Their actions are completely antithetical to a people who broadcast warning to us all these years."

"Are they somehow a species who says the opposite of what they mean?" asked the General.

"I don't see how. If that was the case, Hell, sneak up on us. The chances of Earth realizing those large rocks were starships is remote. At least not until they were about a year out. No warning, no reason to build craft like the ARTHUR C. CLARKE."

"You mean an automated battlecruiser rather than explorers."

"Yes. If Earth II had exploded without the

warnings, we would still be trying to figure out what happened."

Bob, Chauncy, and the General sat in the communications room as everyone tried to figure out the disjointed signals coming from the Good Folk. The anti-matter engines were warmed up. Half of the fifty crew members were aboard to service the engines and weapon systems. They were now the most important humans in orbit of Pluto.

"What do you have, Doctor?" Samara asked.

"I am trying to piece together some partial messages. The so-called Good Folk are talking on each ship among themselves, using smells and local gestures, so all I have are visual images between the starships."

"So what do you see, love?" asked Bob.

"They tried to deflect the smashed shuttle but were only partially successful. General, did you have some additional munitions aboard the assault shuttle?"

"Yes. A couple of old fashioned shape charges attached to drones, in case we had to try to breach from a distance. Then the Marines would have to..."

"Make a Flying Monkey assault, in their combat suits," interjected Bob. "And hope they don't go spinning off into space."

"I forget, Robert, you're a combat veteran."

"So, someone decided to ram them instead."

"That was Lt. Perez. Gutsy move. She'll go far."

"Well, Bob, General, the smashed shuttle exploded and sent the equivalent of a meteor shower onto the nearest starship. There were casualties."

"Brought that on themselves," stated the General.

"No argument here. But, well, I get some confusing visual signals, transmissions, maybe some of it aimed at us."

The General frowned as she spoke.

"What kind of chatter is it?"

"They keep transmitting visual images of 'You/ They... Were/Are Warning. Danger.' Then a picture of what looks like a figurine."

"Please show us."

Chauncy pulled up one of the transmitted visuals. When Bob saw it, he said, "Aw, shit."

"What is it, love?" Chauncy asked.

"That image? That is a straight out of pictures of figures, statues from the Babylonian and Sumerian empires. Those beings depicted with the horned crowns were gods or godlike beings, often referred to as the Anunnaki."

"Well, maybe they intercepted some old television educational broadcast."

"And decide to make a big deal out of these images? Out of the millions of broadcasts and pictures floating around, they make a big deal about this, about a race they have never met."

"I don't see the point," said the General.

"The point is that there has been over a hundred years of speculation based on various translations of Sumerian texts that the Anunnaki were a race of beings from off-world, aliens who came to Earth thousands of years ago. They came to mine our planet for gold and other resources, and some say made US, Homo sapiens to be their slaves. Some people said they interbred with us."

"This mythology means what?"

"The Anunnaki were the original badasses. They fought great wars among themselves and involved our ancestors. They had space travel, which meant they could fight wars in space."

"But its all based on supposition and myth," said Chauncy.

"Then why would an alien non-humanoid care about it? Think on that. They were trying to figure out who we were. Someone panicked, jump the gun, and found out the hard way that, yes, we can make war in space."

The two women stared at Bob.

"Don't you see? We have met the enemy, and he is us. They were trying to warn us, about these badasses who left a bunch of old munitions around. From thousands of years ago." Bob paused for a moment, then continued.

"Sumerians were horny bastards also. Maybe they got all that sexual proclivity from ancient Anunnaki teachings. At least they were shaped like us. Those slugs were trying to match us up to what they knew about the Anunnaki, and what happened, which was a space war."

"And you say they did?" Asked his wife.

"Why else travel we don't know for sure how many lightyears to run some tests on some upright apes. They were afraid we are the Second Coming. And it is not about a good guy from Nazareth."

The three humans sat silent. Then a communication technician cut in.

"Ma'am, the Aliens just tight beamed us an image."

"Put it up on the screens," said the General

In a moment, a message in block letters appeared.

"WE LEAVE. NO HURT US."

The General snorted in disgust.

"They abuse some humans trying to communicate, and now ask for mercy."

"I still think it was a mistake, General," said Chauncy.

"Yeah, well, maybe their ancestors fought ours. We only have their limited word about what happened. So they best run and hide." Samara turned towards a crewman standing by and spoke.

"First Officer."

"Yes, Ma'am."

"Plot a following course. We need to make sure those 'Slugs' leave our Solar System."

"Yes, Ma'am."

"Robert, Chauncy. Go rest up. It's a military mission now." Samara Kravitz stood with her hands clasped behind her, as many a ships commander had done. The Renfroes headed back to their quarters. As the General had said, it was a Space Command matter now.

The two lovers laid in each others arms in their bed, finding a sense of well-being in the arms of another human.

"Well, Chauncy. Two positive things resulted from this...mess."

"What's that, Bob?"

"Well, we know how to screw in Zero G for one."

"What's the other?"

"You didn't cut off my dick like some slugs do to each other."

"Not yet, my dear," Chauncy answered with a grin. "Just piss this Ginger off and see what happens."

"You are so mean, Saucy."

"Yeah, but you still love me, Bob."

"Yes. So kiss me, my dear, before the mode escapes us."

"One last thing. Bob."

"What's that Saucy."

"I'll never look at escargot the same again."

The humans then performed an act seemingly unique to Homo sapiens who had faced danger.

They laughed.

Always Read
the Instruction Manual

Lauren Patzer

S o, I said 'Not the red one,'" Dr. Adam Vasillius snickered to the HR administrator who flashed her bright white teeth as she giggled. Her eyes twinkled and he smiled as she tossed her bleach blonde hair over one shoulder.

Suddenly, the door opened and a harried ginger man in a lab coat sighed in relief.

"Thank God!" the man said.

Adam rolled his eyes as the blonde smiled and then looked back at the computer monitor she was working on. She began typing and ignored him. Adam turned around to see his lab assistant, Danny, standing there looking flushed. He was clearly out of breath and held onto the door handle for support.

"For goodness sake, man, pull yourself together," Adam said as he walked out the door past Danny.

Danny gulped and turned to follow him.

"You need to come down to the lab," Danny said.

"And see what's on the slab?" Adam responded and then frowned. His lab assistant was likely too young to get the Rocky Horror reference. "Seriously, what is it? I was on break."

"Your brother was looking for your Netflix password," Danny said.

"Not surprising. Although, I did think the Rubik's cube would keep him occupied until he figured out how to take it apart. Did he cut himself on the scissors in my desk?"

"No, but he was looking through your desk and he found the paperwork on artifact 2307." Danny was breathing normally now. Adam thought about speeding up just to keep Danny out of breath, but he needed to hear the full story no matter how mind numbing it might be.

"He couldn't understand what it was anymore than we could." Adam ran his hand through his thick black hair. He could feel a migraine coming on which normally accompanied all his interactions with his brother. "I don't understand why 'bring your brother' to work day became a thing. Tell you what, you take care of my brother and I'm going back to ask Melanie why they made it a priority."

Adam turned to walk back to the HR administrator he'd just been flirting with. Danny grabbed his arm.

"Your brother's a slug," Danny said.

"Well, I could've told you that. I don't think he's worked a day in his life. Mother coddles him so," Adam said.

"No, I mean he interacted with the artifact and it turned him into a slug," Danny said.

Adam grabbed his pocket and felt the security card missing.

"Of all the—okay, let's go," Adam said and led Danny down the three floors to the basement, instructing Danny to use his security card at each level since Adam's was missing. On the way, Adam passed several women who winked at him and he smiled briefly, but quickly resumed his scowl when they'd passed from view.

Upon reaching the basement, they walked down the hall and into the secured room surrounded by reinforced concrete walls three feet thick. After passing through the security door, Adam gasped at a six foot long, three foot thick slug sitting by the control panel across the room. Just beyond the control panel, a five foot long, purple, glowing rectangular staff with alien markings on it sat upon a long table. Robotic arms hovered over the surface; one of them touched the center of the staff.

"Control, update," Adam said out loud.

"What the hell, there's two of you?" a voice replied

over the intercom.

"Sylvester, I should've known it'd be you not monitoring the artifact," Adam replied.

"Well, Dr. Vasillius, it just so happens you walked in here a few moments ago and a giant slug appeared in your place. Clearly, you accessed some type of transporter beam," Sylvester replied. "What did you do?"

"That was my brother who walked in here moments ago. Is the translator working?" Adam asked.

"Uh, yes." There was an audible click. "It's working fine."

Adam sighed and looked at the slug. "Evan, you've never looked better." The slug raised its head and moved its grimy antennae.

"Adam, what kind of stupid thing did your magic stick do to me?" Evan's voice asked over the loud speaker.

"Well, dear brother, who should have stayed in my office where I put you..." Adam started, glaring at the slug. "We didn't know what it would do which is why we have touched any of the surfaces except for the unmarked edges where it was safe to touch."

"I just wanted to see if it sparked," Evan replied over the loud speaker. The slug moved slowly toward a couch near the rear of the room.

"It appears to have changed the operator into the

thing it most resembles," Adam said. "Does this help us with the translation?"

Adam looked back at the small glass sliver behind him where the two controllers sat behind thick bullet proof glass. There was a click.

"Dr. Antonov here," a woman's voice announced. "Given the possible combinations of translations, we're trying to narrow it down now. It appears to be trans-something. Perhaps transmutation, transreality, or something of that nature. The computers are still crunching the numbers."

"Fantastic." Evan's voice came over the loud speaker. Adam glanced back at the slug. "Tell me when you find the undo button."

"Or perhaps we could just bring in some salt shakers for a picnic?" Adam retorted. The slug quivered.

"Mother will hear about this!" Even responded as his antennae whirled rapidly over his translucent gray head.

"Not if she doesn't come down here where the translator is," Danny chimed in and then cringed as Adam gave him a withering glare. "Sorry, just trying to help."

"OK, while my brother the slug here hasn't consumed any particulate matter yet, there may still be a chance to bring him back with no ill effects. Do we see anything resembling reverse or the infamous undo in the symbols?"

"Dr. Vasillius," Dr. Antonov said. "There may not be a reversal function. Scrambling DNA to a particular life form is one thing, maintaining the cerebral patterns for intelligent thought resembling the original subject is another incredible feat. A simple undo function may not exist or worse yet may just scramble him into a different form. At some point he may lose all intellectual identity and sense of humanity."

A strange sticky mucous sound erupted from the slug. Evan was eating the couch.

"May not matter after all," Adam said. "The subject has started consuming matter."

"This couch is delicious!" Evan said over the loud speaker.

"So," Sylvester responded. "If this reacts to the user's controls..."

Suddenly the robotic arms started touching the staff all over. Thousands of light beams shot out through the walls. Just as suddenly, they stopped.

"Technician Grinnell initiated a connection to the internet," Dr. Antonov said over the intercom. "His last action caused him to be transformed into a weasel. I've cut the connection to the internet. Trying to reestablish normal function."

The robotic arms moved away from the surface of the artifact.

"We're probably going to lose our funding over this," Adam mumbled.

"Oh," Danny said. "Look at this. The internet connection recorded the various beams effects and it appears that's given the translator program a bit of a boost!"

Danny ran over the control panel and directed one of the robotic arms into place.

"See this?" Danny asked excitedly.

Adam walked over to be closer to the artifact.

"The translator says this should be Regression," Danny said. "If we point it right at the word,"

Danny moved the robotic arm into place as Evan slowly moved behind him. Danny stepped back, touched Evan's slimy surface, shouted out in disgust and fell forward into the controls, pushing the robotic arm into the surface of the artifact. A flash of light shot out from the artifact and Danny disappeared.

"Whoa," Evan said over the speakers. "Looks like Danny regressed to nothing."

Adam looked down at where Danny had been standing. There was a tiny puddle of fluid. He grabbed a magnifying glass from a drawer and peered down at the puddle.

"Too tiny to verify, but I suspect Danny has regressed to either a fertilized egg or an egg and sperm just before they joined together," Adam stood up.

"Shouldn't it have been a few months old fetus

when the heart starts beating?" Evan said over the speakers.

"Really," Adam said. "You've mutated into a primordial slug and you're going to debate abortion ethics with me again?"

"I've always felt you were a little too scientific with your interpretation," Evan replied. "I think there's a time when the soul merges with the fetus and really, what better time than when the heartbeat starts?"

"I'm pretty sure when the embryo can feel pain is more likely the time," Dr. Antonov said over the speakers.

"This is not the time to discuss it!" Adam shouted. "We've possibly lost two people permanently to transmutation and another to regressing to a time before he was born. I'd say we have bigger problems than specific theories on viable fetuses!"

"Egghead," another voice announced over the speaker. There's was a brief squeal and then the sound of a drawer slamming shut.

"That was Sylvester chiming in," Dr. Antonov said. "I pushed him into an open drawer and locked it."

"That's probably for the best," Adam said. He put his hands on his face and then rubbed his eyes. "We need to contact the DoD and let them know what happened."

"Oh, yes, well," Dr. Antonov replied. "They're

actually waiting on the line already. They called us."

"I guess we can take this now." Adam glared at Evan. "You keep your antennae silent."

There were a few audible clicks and a deep voice boomed throughout the room. Adam slapped his hands over his ears.

"Is this thing working? God, I hate technology."

"Adjusting volume," Dr. Antonov said before Adam could ask. "You should be connected now, General."

"About time," the deep voice announced at a much lower volume. "Dr. Vasillius?"

"This is Dr. Adam Vasillius," Adam responded. "To whom am I speaking?"

"This is General Bellman. Do you know what's happening?"

"You rang us," Adam said with a smirk. There was an audible sigh from the General.

"That joke never fails to unimpress, Adam," General Bellman said.

"Thought a little levity might brighten the mood," Adam replied.

"A little levity would," General Bellman replied and cleared his throat. "Now, what the hell's going on down there?"

"We had a small security breach from inside the facility," Adam said. "Seems Sylvester Grinnell thought opening the facility to an internet connection would be a good idea."

"Ahh, Grinnell. President's cousin. Only reason he got the clearance. Kind of a weasel."

"You have no idea," Adam responded.

"Look, Adam. We have reports that the President is missing. He was talking to the Vice President, tweeting about some nonsense, and then the next thing you know, he's gone. Only thing they found was his phone on the floor and what looked like a bran flake sitting on his chair in the oval office."

"Flake?" Adam said, eyebrows raised. "Yeah, that makes sense."

"What's that mean?"

"Look, General, Sylvester did something to the artifact that caused some pretty strange effects. We're trying to get to the bottom of it but... well, it's alien technology. It's going to take some time. I'd suggest trying to preserve the flake very carefully; I'm pretty sure it's the President."

"The President? Well... get hopping, Adam! I'm getting reports that the La Brea Tar Pits are expanding, New York is crumbling like a cracker and Chicago has been turned entirely into cheese. Also, and this isn't verifiable yet, an entire building of Russian hackers in St. Petersburg has been turned into trolls—the big, green club wielding kind."

Evan made a grotesque sound and excreted a dark slimy fluid from beneath his mantle.

"Sorry," Evan said. "Didn't know I had to go."

"Who needs to go?" General Bellman demanded.

"We need to go and continue our analysis right away, General," Adam said quickly. He made a throat cutting gesture toward the control booth. A few audible clicks and there was silence.

"We're disconnected," Dr. Antonov said.

Adam walked over to a sink on the side wall and retched.

"Christ, Evan," Adam said between heaves. "What did you eat?"

"Couch, but that was recently. Might have been the eggs Benedict I had this morning. Maybe the sushi I had last night," Evan said as he slowly crawled along on his foot toward Adam. "Hard to say, really. I'm not sure how the digestive track works in a human. I can't imagine how it works as a slug."

"Dr. Vasillius, the results are in from the translation routines on the artifact," Dr. Antonov interrupted. "However, while I can say we've identified what most of the functions are, it doesn't really put us on the trail of undoing the damage."

"Well," Adam replied as he sat down on a rolling chair and slid up to a computer. "If we put Chicago and New York together, we'll solve world hunger for a week. Other than that, I got nothing."

Evan oozed back over to the couch and resumed his feast.

"They should make these with wooden pegs instead of nails. The bitter taste is awful." Evan voice echoed through the room as Adam typed away madly on the computer in front of him.

"I'll be sure to mention that when we order a new couch," Adam replied as he sat back in the chair. "It's no use. This doesn't give us a big enough data set to fully translate the rest of the artifact."

"That's a bummer," Evan replied as his mass dropped to the ground with a wet plop. "Too bad you don't have an instruction manual."

"Maybe we do," Dr. Antonov said. "Accessing the other artifacts recovered from the dig site now."

"Of course!" Adam shouted. "We run the translation matrix across the other artifacts and see if we can decipher more of the code and maybe even locate an instruction manual!"

"You didn't try that before?" Evan said as he climbed up onto the remaining piece of the sofa. "And you call yourself scientists. Wow."

"We haven't tried it since we got the additional data. With a fuller key, we should be able to unlock more and possibly expand the key even further," Adam said.

"Clearly I'm the brains in the family," Evan replied as he munched on upholstery. "That's why mom likes me better."

"Oh please, Evan," Adam replied as he held his

head. The impending migraine was taking hold. "Mother likes you because you live at home, file down her corns and shave her back."

"Somebody's gotta do it!" Evan replied as he dug into the wooden frame in the middle of the partially collapsed couch.

"Guys, please," Dr. Antonov said. "This is an open mike and I'm queasy enough as it is watching a giant slug eat couch while millions of people have been turned into cheese and crackers."

Evan stopped eating and his eye stalks looked in the direction of the control panel.

"Hey, weren't you and Danny a thing? Sorry about that," Evan said and then returned his concentration to spitting out brass tacks. They dropped wetly to the ground.

"Yes, well, it wasn't serious anyway," Dr. Antonov sniffed.

"Still," Adam replied. "That does free up your Friday nights now, if you know what I mean."

"Honestly, Dr. Vasillius? Flirting at a time like this?" Dr. Antonov said. He could feel her glaring through the control booth window.

"Just trying a bit of levity," Adam said as he shrugged and slid back to the computer keyboard.

"Your levity could use a lot of work," she responded. There was an audible beep in the background of Dr. Antonov's words. "It looks like the translation routines have completed."

"Really?" Evan said as he gulped down a chunk of wood. "How did it finish that fast?"

"We have three supercomputers in the lower basement processing all the digitized symbols from the artifact trove," Dr. Antonov responded without considering if Evan had the proper security clearance. Adam shook his head.

"Three supercomputers?" Evan raised the top portion of his mucous covered body to stare at the control booth window. "And you can't get a decent chicken salad sandwich in the cafeteria? You brainiacs really have your priorities messed up."

Evan dropped back down and the remainder of the couch collapsed beneath his bulk.

"Oopsie," Evan said and then pulled another strip of upholstery off the rapidly disappearing furniture.

"I shudder to think of what you'll find appetizing after you're done with the sofa," Adam sneered.

"Well, you could let me outside into the picnic area—there's some delicious looking shrubs by the tables," Evan replied.

"Oh," Adam said as he stood up. "I'd like nothing more than to let you leave so you could be properly ah-salted!"

"Cruel, bro," Even said and crawled off the furniture remains, leaving a trail of slime behind him. "It's not my fault your stupid artifact did this!"

"You filed through my desk, stole an access card and broke into this secure facility!"

"Well, I wouldn't have bothered if you hadn't left handwritten notes on the artifact paperwork describing the symbols on the bottom of the shaft as likely seduction or virility runes!" Evan shouted back, antennae whirling angrily.

"Really, Dr. Vasillius?" Dr. Antonov asked.

"Levity!" Adam shouted and sat back down in the chair. "You said we had a translation?"

"Yes," she said and cleared her throat. "According to tablets retrieved just meters away from the shaft, the effects of the artifact are temporary maintained by a cycling quantum field and can be reversed by resetting the object."

"Hot damn!" Evan shouted.

"And how do we reset the object?" Adam asked.

"It looks like... oh, that's interesting. A man and a slug need to have sex on top of the artifact," Dr. Antonov said.

"Not good," Evan replied.

"Natasha!" Adam shouted.

"Levity, Dr. Vasillius," Dr. Antonov chuckled. "The top and bottom of the artifact must be pressed simultaneously to reset the quantum field."

"All right," Adam said getting up from the chair. "Before we do this, get security to take the weasel into custody. Just lock him up in a room."

"Stand by. This will take a few minutes," Dr. Antonov said and the speakers went silent again.

"So," Evan said. "You really think this will work?"

Adam regarded his slug brother for a few seconds.

"I certainly hope so. Lord knows I don't want to be helping mother with her personal hygiene."

"Aww, it's not that bad. She always bakes me cookies afterwards."

"Sounds nice." Adam glanced at the mostly destroyed and consumed couch. "You know, you just ate a couch. That could present a problem."

"Well," Evan replied. "I've got like a billion teeth, so it's pretty well chewed."

"OK," Dr. Antonov said over the speakers. "Let's get this party started."

"Umm," Adam replied. "Maybe we could delay it a bit. I mean, Evan here just ate a couch."

"Dr. Vasillius... Evan... the President is a bran flake who could break into tiny pieces at any moment and more people are disappearing into a pool of expanding, boiling tar every minute we delay. Chicago and New York are literally getting consumed with each passing second."

Adam looked at his slug brother with a tear in his eye.

"Hey," Evan said. "If anything bad happens, you'll take care of mom, right?"

"You know I will." Adam nodded. He stood up and

walked to the console.

"Um, I got it," Dr Antonov said. "Computer controlled to do it simultaneously."

"Right," Adam said and backed away from the console. He glanced back at his brother. "See you on the other side."

Evan's eye stalks waved.

"Here we go," Dr. Antonov said. The robotic arms moved slowly to each end of the artifact. Lasers lit up on either side so they could accurately measure the distance to time the simultaneous touch perfectly.

Adam couldn't bring himself to look behind him as the arms moved in and a bright light bathed the entire room. He closed his eyes and grimaced when he heard Evan cry out in pain. There was a sickening popping sound followed by a loud thump. The accompanying silence scared him more than anything he'd ever experienced. To his left, the desiccated body of Danny appeared.

"Adam," Dr. Antonov said quietly. "I'm so sorry."

Adam turned around for a quick glance, saw the horror before him and quickly turned back.

"As I am for you," Adam said nodding at Danny's body on the floor. "You know, my brother's the last person on earth I would have imagined to give his life so others could live."

Made in the USA
Columbia, SC
02 October 2021